ABOUT
THE
B'NAI
BAGELS

ABOUT THE B'NAI BAGELS

written & illustrated
by E. L. KONIGSBURG

ATHENEUM　　　NEW YORK

FOR MY OWN DEAR MOTHER
who knows almost nothing
about baseball and
almost everything
about love
&
stuffed cabbage

ATHENEUM
MACMILLAN PUBLISHING COMPANY
866 THIRD AVENUE, NEW YORK, NY 10022
COLLIER MACMILLAN CANADA, INC.

PRINTED IN THE UNITED STATES OF AMERICA

FIRST EDITION
11 13 15 17 19   20 18 16 14 12

LIBRARY OF CONGRESS CATALOG CARD NUMBER 69-13529
ISBN 0-689-20631-3

ABOUT
THE
B'NAI
BAGELS

1

UP UNTIL OCTOBER OF LAST YEAR MY MOTHER HAD
two hobbies: major league baseball and my brother,
Spencer. Spencer was her great year-round activity
and baseball was seasonal. Don't get the idea that I
was neglected, because I wasn't. It's just that Spencer
is a lot older than I, and Mother had a lot more years
to specialize in him. Actually, she raised us like two
only children. Especially Spencer.

Last October, Spencer, who lived at home with us
in Point Baldwin and who commuted every day to
New York University, began calling our mother
Bessie, and he began arguing with her about everything. Dad said that he was just feeling his oats and
acting sophomoric. Which seems funny because

Spencer was actually a Junior in college at that time. Mom got her feelings terribly hurt just about every day, and she began having long private discussions with Dad about "Where have I gone wrong, Sam?" and "What have I ever done to that boy?" I often listened in because it was quite a bad habit I had, and that was the only way I knew to find out what they might be saying about me in nine years when I would be twenty-one and feeling my own oats.

Dad who was very busy at the time—Dad being an accountant and being that he was starting some new big accounts—told Mother to be thankful that Spencer was not a hippie; he still wore socks. He advised her to wait a few months for this phase to pass, see a psychiatrist, or get some new interests.

Mom was too impatient to wait past Election Day. She refused to take it lying down. On a psychiatrist's couch or anywhere. So she started a herb garden, but the plants got sick, and all of Mom's loving care, fertilizer, and chicken soup couldn't make them well. They died in February, which is rather a doldrums kind of a month anyway, and Mom was feeling defeated again. Too bad it happened just then because in another two months the major leagues would have begun their season, and she would not have wanted to go to that meeting of the B'nai B'rith Sisterhood and get entangled in baseball in Little League in the way that she did. A way that invaded my privacy and might have declared practically the last little piece of my life as occupied territory.

In a normal February, Mother would have noted the meeting on her calendar and then forgotten about it. She would have stayed at home making stuffed cabbage, as she was doing that Wednesday when Spencer walked into the kitchen and mentioned that he had been to some famous Hungarian restaurant in New York and had ordered their stuffed cabbage, which was delicious because it had raisins in it and why didn't Mother try it that way?

"Raisins in stuffed cabbage?" she asked casually at first.

"Yeah, it's good. Sort of sweet and sour," he answered.

"Raisins in stuffed cabbage? Never. Sauerkraut, I put in my stuffed cabbage. Sauerkraut and a touch of sugar."

Spencer snapped at her, "You see, Bessie, that's what's wrong with you. You'll never try anything new. Your mind is closed."

Mother snapped back, "I happen to like my own stuffed cabbage. With sauerkraut. That makes my mind closed?"

"No. But the raisins is symbolic. The raisins *are* symbolic. You're resistant to change. What's so important about stuffed cabbage that you shouldn't be willing to change it?"

"You want to know what's so important about stuffed cabbage? I'll tell you what's so important. It takes two and a half hours of my life to make it. That's what's so important. Every time, two and one half hours."

"I'll tell you how to cut down on that amount of time," Spencer shouted.

"How? By putting raisins in?"

"No. By cutting me out. Don't make my portion." And with that, he slammed the kitchen door except that you can't really slam it; it's louvered and on hinges so the two sides just kept flapping back and forth.

Mother yelled after the flapping doors, "No one tells Heinz how to make ketchup, and no one tells Bessie Setzer how to stuff cabbage." Turning to me, she asked, "You, Mark, you like the way I make stuffed cabbage?"

"What's not to like?" I answered. Really, I thought, if it was as unimportant as Spencer told Mother it was, then why was it important enough to have her change? It was obvious that Spencer was becoming grown-up; he didn't make sense.

"When I think of all the hours of stuffed cabbage I put into that boy. Wasted. Just wasted." Mom was holding a slotted spoon and addressing God. Up until the time I began Sunday School, I thought that He lived in the light fixture on our kitchen ceiling. "Raisins are raisins, and cabbage is cabbage," she mumbled into the pot. Then she jabbed the spoon into the air and announced, "And in my pot they won't meet."

She stirred some more and continued talking to the pot, "A twenty-one year-old boy who doesn't know enough to pick up his dirty socks or hang up his pajamas suddenly becomes Mr. Ladies' Home Journal. Illustrated." And without looking up from the pot she added, "Mark, hurry or you'll be late for Hebrew School."

Some days it seemed as if the only conversation I had with my mother was *be-lated*. Like "Eat now, Moshe, or you'll *be late* for school." Or "Get dressed already, or you'll *be late* for synagogue." Once she even said to me, "Mark, go wash your hair now, or you'll be late for combing." I still haven't figured that one out. Last year there was so much be-lated conversation in our house that you could actually call it nagging. That was because last year in addition to everything else, I was seriously in the business of being Hebrew, being that I was twelve years old and preparing for my Bar Mitzvah. Bar Mitzvah marks the time you become thirteen years old and can participate as an adult in all the religious services at the synagogue. Preparing for it starts when a guy is eight years old, but the volume is kept soft and low and part-time. Then, BLAST—the commercial comes on when you reach the age of twelve. And in your twelfth year you become devoted. Devoted to lessons on Sunday morning until it becomes Sunday afternoon, and afternoon lessons on Mondays and Wednesdays. Afternoons until 7:00 at night. According to my mother I was always about to *be late* for one or the other of those devotions.

She never remembered that I needed five minutes less than I had before to get to the synagogue because I didn't meet Hersch any more.

Hersch means Herschel Miller. He and I used to be good friends before his family sold their house two blocks from ours and bought one up on Crescent Hill. Crescent Hill once was a huge estate; someone divided it into lots with houses that were bigger and that looked less alike than the houses in our section of town. All the kids from there went to the Crescent Hill School for the elementary and junior high grades, but they funneled back into our district for senior high. Even in high school, though, they kept a little bit apart from the rest of the kids. I remember Spencer talking about it when he was in high school; they were called the Crescent Hill Mob. Their mothers were always busy with referendums and such to get their own senior high, but something kept stopping the referendums. I think it was fathers. The Mob mixed with us in high school. Some also mixed in Hebrew School. But not thoroughly. They always separated off into car pools when Hebrew was over. In our part of town we walked.

From third grade through sixth, before Hersch moved, ever since we began Hebrew lessons on a normal twice-a-week basis, Hersch and I would walk home from public school together, would dump our books, would grab something to eat, and would meet on the corner of King and Chestnut. We had two great things going for us: time and geography. We had the same schedules: public school, Hebrew School, Sunday School. And we lived only two blocks from each other. Besides that, we liked some of the same things. I liked baseball more, and last year I talked Hersch into trying out for Little League; he became a pretty good player. Once I had to talk him into seeing a James Bond movie, and he went back twice. Paid each time. And he never missed a James Bond movie after that even though I did.

Sometimes I thought that Hersch was more of a brother to me than Spencer. We each had some bumps in our personalities, but they were in different places and at least they were the same size. That made it good; you need a friend who is a little different from you to rub against. That way you file down each other's rough edges.

I never thought that Hersch's moving would make a difference, but it did. By February the only times we saw each other were official times. Like at services or lessons. Besides time and distance, there was something else that got in the way of our friendship; someone else—Barry Jacobs. Barry lived up on Crescent Hill, too, near Hersch. There had been no one to take Hersch's place for me. Hersch had moved over Labor Day; as everyone knows, the year begins right after that. Years move from left to right from September to January and from right to left from January to June; June through August is a hook that links up to next September. Comes September of a Bar Mitzvah year, a guy doesn't have much leftover time for social life. Making friends from scratch takes time for walking places together or running over to each other's house to check on the homework assignment. The kind of time I didn't have.

So on that fatal night in February, that night of the raisin fight, I walked to and from Hebrew School alone. It was dark before I came from lessons to supper with stuffed cabbage and without Spencer. That makes a quiet meal. Not like chicken soup with crackers and Spencer.

"Mark," Mom said, "you clear the table and put the dishes into the dishwasher. I have to go to Sisterhood."

"I have homework," I replied.

"Another one to sass me back!" She was talking to the Deity again. Then she returned to earth and addressed me. "Is it too much to ask to have you clear the table so that I can get out of the house for a few hours?"

"O.K., I'll do it," I said.

"For a few hours. And it's not even recreation. It's for you, Mark, that I go to these meetings."

"I said that I would do it."

"Don't do me any favors!" she said as she began banging the dishes around and stacking them into the dishwasher.

I looked at Dad and shrugged. "All I said was that I would do it."

"Go, Bessie," Dad said. "Go to the meeting. I'll clear up the dishes." And he got up, and *he* began rinsing dishes and putting them into the dishwasher, too.

In no time at all, the dishes were done.

As Mother was leaving, I called to her, "Have a good time."

"Who can have a good time with that bunch of biddies?" Mother replied. She often referred to the B'nai B'rith Sisterhood as her Biddie Club.

"Then why are you going?" I asked.

"I told you why I'm going. For a few hours I am going. Because you have to go *out* to have *out*side interests. Your father and your Aunt Thelma say that I need outside interests."

And so it was because of Spencer and a bunch of dead herbs that Mother went to Sisterhood to get outside interests and as a result she moved into and organized another corner of my life. But it wasn't until later that I wished there had been a good movie for her to go to that night instead.

The next morning I was eating breakfast when Mother came into the kitchen. Spencer never ate breakfast, a habit that my mother could not adjust to altogether. In fact, if my mother could rewrite the

Ten Commandments, one of them would be "Thou shalt eateth of breakfast." She talked to the ceiling about it a great deal. "You would think that a boy with his education would know that he has to have some food in his stomach to lubricate it. Otherwise, ulcers he'll get. From the empty walls rubbing together. *Peristalsis*, you named it, dear God." Then to Spencer she'd explain, "So help me, Spencer, if you come down with a case of the ulcers, don't look to me for a cream diet. It's all I can do to satisfy . . ." There was usually more to her little speech, but none of it was necessary this morning. Spencer was foraging in the refrigerator for things he usually wouldn't even look at before noon. With or without raisins.

"How many in your class, Mark?" Mother asked me, making sure that Spencer was listening. I didn't much like it when she was mad at Spencer and used me as a bank board to bounce questions to him.

"Twenty-seven," I answered.

"Good," she said. "I want you to tell the whole class to try out for the Little League team. This year Sisterhood is sponsoring."

"They can't all try out," I explained.

"Anyone who won't be thirteen until after August 1 is eligible. There aren't any left-backers in your class. They can all try out."

"Mother," I said, "they don't call it 'left back' anymore. They call it 'retained.' "

"Whatever they are called, there aren't any in

your class, and I want they should all try out. The Sisterhood is sponsoring."

"They can't all try out," I repeated.

I could tell that Mother didn't want to be drawn into an argument with me because there was nothing that could make Spencer lose interest in a conversation faster than one of Mother's arguments with me. But Mother couldn't resist getting answers. "Why?"

"Because fourteen of them are girls."

The information registered. But Mother wanted to get back to Spencer. There was some message she had to get across to him. The passwords seemed to be *the Sisterhood is sponsoring,* which she said now very loudly.

"The Sisterhood is sponsoring."

Spencer finally asked. "What happened to the B'nai B'rith Men's Club?"

"Did you say something, Spencer?" Mother asked innocently.

"Yes, I did. I asked what happened to the B'nai B'rith Men's Club?"

"Nothing happened. They're still there. Meeting the last Thursday of every month."

"I mean," he said, swallowing a huge wad of onion roll, "how come they're not sponsoring the team?"

"Management problems they've got."

"What's that mean?" Spencer closed his eyes and said slowly, "C'mon, Bessie, don't be coy. I haven't got all day."

"What's coy about management problems? They've got no manager."

"So who—whom?—does Sisterhood have?"

Mother's eyes grew big and with a hitchhiker's thumb she pointed to her cheek, smiled, and said, "Me whom. That's whom."

"You!" Spencer shrieked. "That is the end! The absolute end!" And he banged his hand on the table. Too bad he had just taken the tomato juice out of the refrigerator.

I ran to get the paper towels, but Mother and Spencer hardly noticed. The juice was plip-plipping onto his Hush Puppy size twelves. I scooted under the table to wipe up. I lifted first one foot and then the other and wiped all around. And he just kept stamping his feet.

"It's against regulations. No girls allowed." Stamp. Stamp. Hush Puppy size twelves.

"No girl *players.* Doesn't say anything about managers." Stamp. Stamp. Lazy Bones bedroom slippers size eight double A.

Splatter. Stamp. Hush Puppies: "Where will you women stop? Why can't you stay in the kitchen?"

Stamp. Tap. Tap. Lazy Bones slippers: "And do what? Make rotten stuffed cabbage?"

I rinsed out the sponge and was finishing up the tomato juice when Spencer swept his hand along the table and caused it to rain down peanut butter, cream cheese, and five bagels.

"No one said that your stuffed cabbage was rotten. I said that your mind was closed."

I rescued three bagels and took a fourth, coated with cream cheese and soaked in the rest of the tomato juice to the garbage. Then I sat down to await the conclusion.

"My mind is closed? Listen who's talking." She was conferring with the ceiling again. "Listen who's talking, will You, dear God? The boy who just said that women should stay in the kitchen thinks that he has an open mind."

"All right, Bessie. Let's discuss this calmly. Just you and me. Leave Him out of it," Spencer added, lifting his eyebrows toward the ceiling.

They sat down opposite each other at the kitchen table. Mother propped her chin into her hand and her elbow into a puddle of tomato juice. That began more plip-plipping; I ignored it.

Spencer sat down, too, and continued. "What, may I ask, do you know about baseball?"

Mother appealed to the light fixture again. "He's asking me, Bessie Setzer, what I know about baseball. I, who—whom?—who never miss a Mets home game. I, who am practically a walking encyclopedia of baseball facts. He asks *me* what *I* know about baseball." Spencer reached across the table and put his hand under Mother's chin to lower it. Mother looked at her elder son and said, "Shame on you, Spencer. Shame."

Spencer had about as much patience with shame talk as he had with one of Mother's arguments with me. "So, Bessie, you're a fan. That's all you've told me. You've got a good record of attendance at Ladies' Day. Nothing else." Mother began to interrupt, but Spencer raised his hands, palms outward in front of his face. "No, Bessie, you've merely told me that you are a fan. In words of one syllable, you are a baseball fan. Not a manager."

"Baseball has two syllables, and manager has three," I said.

"And you, Mark, you have bad manners," he snapped.

"Yes," Mother said, "don't interrupt your college brother's bad manners with your own." Then to Spencer she added, "You giving him lessons in manners is like you giving me lessons in stuffed cabbage."

"Or like you giving lessons in baseball!" Spencer answered.

Mother got up from the table and standing full height with just the tips of her fingers resting on the table reminded, "Watch it, Spencer, I'm about to lose my temper."

"Well, tell me just one thing you know about baseball management, Bessie. Not baseball. Baseball management."

Mother looked at me and then at Spencer. "I know where to get lots of free advice." And out she marched.

Her toe caught in the last bagel on the floor. She stooped down, picked it up and zoomed it over her shoulder. It hit the garbage bag square on. Without looking back at it, she smiled to Spencer and to me and marched upstairs lifting her housecoat ever so slightly. Like a queen.

Spencer yelled after her, "It's not basketball you'll be coaching, you know."

Mother didn't answer.

2

FOR A SHORT TIME FOLLOWING MOTHER'S ANNOUNCE-
ment there was frantic peace in our house. Almost no
arguments. But there was almost no conversation either. Dad was elbow deep in tax accounts; Spencer
was finishing a research paper; Mother was attending
meetings, meetings, meetings. We seemed to eat out
of cans and in shifts during those weeks, but I didn't
especially mind. My thoughts on the subject at that
time were: after all, not every guy could have a
mother as a manager. Until she had made her an-
nouncement, I wasn't even sure that I'd join the team
this year. The B'nai B'rith had been a loser. It had
gotten pretty depressing toward the end of the season. The scores sounded more like football: 14-0, 21-

3, with us always on the single digit end. We had won two games all year. Both against the Sears Roebucks. One was by forfeit. The Sears manager had a violent disagreement with the umpire and hadn't remembered until after his first punch that he was supposed to have been teaching gung-ho good sportsmanship. And to take the edge off those wins—the Sears Roebucks had been the next-to-bottom team.

Actually last season was worse than depressing; it was boring. Our manager and coach were out of town on business over half the time. Our team ended up under the thumbs of the few guys like Barry Jacobs who could handle the ball. Guys like Barry refused to give ordinary type players a break. Myself, being an ordinary type player, resented it. If my mother went to meetings and was made manager this year, I figured I would have a chance. And maybe a little bit better than just a chance. I had visions of helpful practice sessions in our yard before supper.

During this time, our days of stuffed cabbage and roast chicken were over, and up until the night of the tomato soup, I felt that it was going to be worth it.

The night of the tomato soup:

That night for supper I received a can of Campbell's Old-fashioned Tomato Rice Soup, a can opener, and a note:

Moshe darling—

Mother is at meeting. Please split this with Dad.
There's some leftover tuna salad in the refrig.

*God and Sisterhood willing, I'll see you and the
kitchen, which you've made immaculately spot-
less, sometime around eight.*

> *Love,*
> *Mom*

That was nothing unusual lately. Dad and I split
the soup. I put some in a bowl for him, and I spooned
mine right out of the pot. Dad didn't notice until he
asked for seconds, and I lifted my spoon and began
to pour more into his bowl.

"We're out of soup bowls?" he asked.

"No," I answered.

"Why then are you eating out of the pot?"

"Because it saves dirtying dishes," I answered.

"Why become a savage? How much more work
is it to use one more dish?" He was growing impatient.

So was I. I was getting fed up, and it wasn't with
good cooking. "It takes only one dish per person to
make a stack, and it seems that I'm always elected to
clean up the stack."

"My dear young man," Dad started.

I wasn't in the mood for that, so I interrupted,
"Listen, Dad," I said, "you're not going to like this,
but . . . but if you want restaurant service, why don't
you take us to one." And then I mumbled, "Or fly
United." I lost. He heard it.

He turned almost as red as Campbell's Old-fashioned Tomato Rice Soup. "You may finish your

soup, Mark, and you may finish your tuna fish salad, Mark. And you may also clean up the kitchen. Then you may go to bed. I don't want another word out of you."

"What about my homework?" I asked.

"Did I say 'not another word?' I'll set the alarm for six o'clock. In your room. You can do your homework at six o'clock in the morning. Now, not another word."

We finished the tuna. I cleaned the kitchen making as much fuss and confusion as I thought I could without bringing Dad out of his office. I figure that I about doubled my work. There wasn't even any Sara Lee stuff in the freezer. No dessert. The whole night was a loser.

I wasn't asleep when Mother came in. What twelve-year-old who hasn't been bitten by a tsetse fly can be asleep at 8:00 p.m.? Besides, I was sore. You can't win with parents. They always have reasons. Even if you, their own flesh and blood child, have reasons as logical as theirs, they have more of them. When she came in, Dad was in the fourth bedroom, the one he calls *office*, Mother calls *den*, and Spencer and the man who sold us the house call *family room*.

"Yoo hoo, Sam, I'm home," she called.

"I'm in the office, Bessie," he answered. "And very busy."

"Where's Mark?" she asked.

"In bed," Dad replied.

"What's the matter? He have a fever or something?" Mom started up the steps. It's not even a full-fledged flight. Our house is split level, so she was at Dad's door in a minute.

"No, he doesn't have a fever. It's a simple case of hot headedness. Not fever."

Mother said, "Oh, O.K. I'll find out about it later. In private." Those two! They were always having private conversations. You'd think they worked for the CIA or something.

Mother popped into my bedroom to kiss me goodnight, but I turned over and buried my face in the pillow. I wasn't in a kissing mood. That had been happening to me a lot lately. Not being in a kissing mood, I mean. All that my mother's trying to become a manager meant to me so far was canned tomato soup, doing dishes, and a goodnight kiss.

As Mother left my room, Spencer walked into the house. You can hear anything that happens everywhere in the house. Or any house on the street. The whole street looks like Monopoly. All the houses alike.

"What's for supper?" Spencer asked.

"I wouldn't know," Mother answered. "In this hotel we don't serve after-theater dinners. The cook leaves at 7:00."

Ha! The cook leaves at 7:00. The cook never appears, I thought as I listened.

"Never mind," Spencer called as his footsteps went toward the refrig. I could tell that Mother was standing by the door, and I could tell that she had her arms crossed over her chest. Her voice always has the sound of crinkling aluminum foil when she stands like that. And her foot was tapping: another sure sign.

"Well, Spencer," Mother began, "I am approved."

"Approved? By Good Housekeeping?"

Her foot was tapping hard now. It set up vibrations. "Spencer, don't be fresh. At last I was approved by the Board of Directors of Little League."

"Congratulations, Bessie. May the best team win," he said. The last was mumbled. Spencer always did talk with his mouth full.

"It's going to be fun. For all of us." Mother's voice was softening.

"Well, it will be interesting. Let's put it that way. But I'm not so sure Mark will enjoy having his mother as manager."

"He'll enjoy. He'll enjoy," she said. Pause. "And so will you enjoy."

"Whether I'll enjoy it or not doesn't matter anyway. I'm out of it. But I might enjoy observing how you manage to manage."

"Spencer, you're going to enjoy more than that. I promise you. You'll enjoy more than that. I've named you coach."

Long silence. Then bang! The refrigerator door.

"Bessie, how could you? I won't do it. I have exams. I have my own social life. I won't do it, Bessie."

"You'll do it, Spencer. You'll do it." Mother's voice was purring.

"Bessie!" Pause. "Mother!" Pause. "Mom!" Pause and louder. "I will not. I cannot."

"Spencer!" Pause. "Son!" Pause. "Boychick!" Pause and softer. "You will. You can."

I heard a chair being pulled out, and from the size of the thud, I guessed that Spencer had just sat down.

Mother then said, "After all, as the saying goes, 'The family that plays together stays together.'"

"Mother, can't you get anything right? It's 'The family that *prays* together, stays together.'"

"So, O.K. We'll do that, too. We'll pray also." I could just see her eyes traveling up toward the ceiling. "Spencer," she continued, "you'll enjoy coaching. You're good at telling other people what to do."

"Mother, I've got school. I've got exams. I've got a social life."

"Yes, Spencer, I hear you. You've also got use of the car. You've also got a generous allowance."

"I need them. How can I commute without them?"

"And I need you, Spencer. How can I manage to manage without you?"

"So what you're telling me is that if I don't coach your team, you are going to take away the car and the allowance."

"Something like that had crossed my mind."

"Aw, Bessie, what the heck kind of psychology is that to raise a son?" Only Spencer didn't say *heck;* he said the other.

Mother answered, "Psychology, it isn't. But it's one heck of a way to get things done." Mother didn't use *heck* either.

3

THERE WAS A MONTH BETWEEN THE TIME MOTHER got approved, and the time tryouts and practices were to begin. The meetings had stopped, and Mother moved back into the kitchen temporarily. Nothing elaborate, and the desserts were store-bought; still I welcomed the change. I was ready for some fringe benefits. I thought that now my mother could take the time to convert me into the Little League Willie Mays. But the weather wouldn't warm up; we had a snowstorm late in March. As long as I can remember, Point Baldwin has always had a snowstorm late in March, and people have always called it "unseasonal." If it happens that time every year, you'd think that they'd call it "seasonal."

28

Early in April we had Passover and Dad was in the worst part of the tax season; both gave him indigestion. We didn't do a lot of the things you're supposed to do for Passover like change dishes and get all the non-Passover foods like flour and cereal out of the house. Mother just put all that stuff into a certain closet and put masking tape around the edges. Once in a while she "borrowed" something from that closet, and by the eighth day the tape looked rather puckered around the edges. Whenever she took something from there, Mother would look up toward the light fixture and say, "begging Your pardon." But we ate matzos instead of bread, which was the most important thing and also the thing that gave Dad his indigestion.

Also Mother made a big Seder and invited her sister, Aunt Thelma and her husband, Uncle Ben. All in all, Passover was casual and fun in our house, but between all the special cooking for that and between all of us having to walk on tiptoes to give Dad peace to work on his accounts, the time for my special help galloped away, and Mother had to get ready for tryouts.

She bought Oaktag and Magic Markers and converted the dining room into a studio. Except it isn't a real dining room. It's around the bend in the living room. Mother calls it a dining area, and Spencer and the man who sold us the house call it a dining el because the living room and the dining room space make an

L shape. The dining area being the short leg of the *L* allowed much of the stuff to pour out into the living room.

The ladies of the Sisterhood came to help Mother. They drank a lot of coffee, smoked a lot of cigarettes, and made posters. One sister marked the margins on the poster board (Lightly, Barbara, lightly. Remember, your lines must be erased.) Another did the lettering, using a template that they bought in the five-and-ten, and a third sister was a specialist in decorating the posters. She drew a boy batting in the upper right and another boy catching in the lower left. (Oh, Lillian, you are so clever!) The ladies complained a lot about the others in Sisterhood. (They certainly want their boys to participate, but they won't lift a finger —not a finger—to help.) Mother didn't complain; she made coffee, emptied ashtrays, and smiled a great deal. You've got to give credit where credit is due.

I came downstairs and leaned over their work; the posters looked the same as they had every year since Point Baldwin had Little League.

ATTENTION
BOYS AGED 9-13
TRYOUTS FOR LITTLE LEAGUE
9-10 years old: Wed. 4:00-6:00
11-12 years old: Thurs. 4:00-6:00
HOLY CHILD PLAYING FIELD
Park and Forest Ave.

"Watch it, Mark!" Mrs. Jacobs scolded. Esther Jacobs was Barry Jacobs' mother, Barry being the guy who my ex-best, Hersch, spent his free time with. "The colors aren't dry yet." I knew Magic Markers dry instantly. It says so right on them. "All I want to do is read it," I answered.

"Wait until next week. They'll be in store windows all over town." And she smiled and looked at the other ladies, not at me.

I put the poster down and read it anyway, without touching it. She kept glancing over at me. I didn't need so much time to read such a little-bitty poster, but I knew that I was making her nervous. I was eating an apple, and I kept taking big crunching bites that sounded as if they'd splat across the whole dining room table. Esther Jacobs turned to look at me and sort-of smiled as I walked around the table. I could tell that I was slowing down production. I left.

"Such a fine boy," she said to my mother. Her saying that was curious because Esther Jacobs did not approve of me. A guy knows when he is being disapproved of; having her not like you makes you feel tarnished. She approved of Hersch. There were times when I thought that my mother should be more like Mrs. Jacobs, calm and interested in stimulating her son. Mrs. Jacobs pronounced words real clearly, too.

Before Hersch had moved, neither of us had liked Barry Jacobs much; we both had thought that Barry

Jacobs was a guy you just couldn't get close to. He had such big personality bumps that they would rub you raw. We used to play the sarcastic game about him. Hersch was great at the sarcastic game. Actually, he was talented at it.

In the sarcastic game we each had our parts—like our friendship. I remember how it went the time that Barry didn't have his Hebrew homework done, before we were in the Bar Mitzvah business, when we had ordinary Hebrew lessons only twice a week. The rabbi kept saying about how if your parents care enough to send you to Hebrew School, and if he cares enough to teach, we should care enough to do our homework. He finished by saying, "We prepare for the larger future of our manhood by preparing for each tomorrow. And if that tomorrow includes homework, prepare it!"

Barry answered, "I'm sorry, Rabbi, but I've been involved in this science project, and I find it so stimulating that I lose track of time."

Everyone knew that Barry had won first prize in the Science Fair in his Crescent Hill school, and he was getting ready to compete in the district Science Fair. Hersch and I sat across from each other, and we exchanged glances. I caught Hersch's eye and raised my eyebrows. That was a signal for us. I can't tell exactly what it meant, but back then we each knew.

Hersch waited for me by the door as we were leaving class, and as soon as we cleared the corridor, we began.

I opened with, "Now tell me, Hairsch, vy iss it zat you don't haf your homevork done?" That was my part: the German accent.

"Well, you see, sir," he responded, falling right in with it. "I got involved."

"Inwolved, yunk man? Inwolved viss vatt?"

"Picking my nose, sir!"

"Unt you considair pickink your nose more shtimulatink zan your homevork?"

"Well, sir, it is not always more stimulating, but there are times when it seems more necessary."

And then Hersch and I would yuk and poke each other as much as carrying our books would allow, and we were home before we knew it.

At first after Hersch moved, we both missed each other a lot. And then it became just me missing him. I didn't notice the first few times he said, "Listen Moshe, I've got to hang up now. I've got to go." I believed that he had to take out the garbage or something. After a few weeks I noticed something else; it was always me who was doing the calling and it was always he who had to go. But I never thought of Barry Jacobs. Not seriously at least, not until one night late in November. It was the night I got disapproved by Mrs. Jacobs. She had phoned my mother and asked if I could come to supper. Only she called it dinner. She mentioned that Hersch was also invited because she "liked Barry to experience all kinds of people." Mrs. Jacobs was very interested in Barry's getting experiences and getting stimulated. My mother was interested in my getting places on time. When my mother asked me if I wanted to go, I wanted to have the courage to say no, but I didn't. Because the truth is that I wanted to see how things were at the Jacobs'. Kind of like the way people would like to know how things are on a family night at Jacqueline Kennedy's without reporters.

My mother drove me there giving me all kinds of hints about using a napkin and not talking with my mouth full. Besides being on time the only thing my mother wanted me to experience was good manners.

After the meal started Mr. Jacobs said, "We left off our discussion of the emerging African nations with an analysis . . ."

I caught Hersch's eye and lifted my eyebrows. He didn't pay attention. I nudged him under the table and did the eyebrow bit again. And all he did was to look at me and look away and say something to Mr. Jacobs about Liberia. The whole meal was pretty uncomfortable, with them trying to get my opinions and me trying to draw conclusions about Africa from having seen four recent Tarzan shows. All of which, I found out later, were filmed in Mexico.

Mrs. Jacob's cooking was like her pronunciation—very tidy. The portions were tiny.

Mrs. Jacobs drove me home. It was a quiet ride; I

could bet that I would get zero for stimulation.
I called Hersch when I got home. "Vat kint of bizness iss zat? Iz alvays dizcussions from Africa at zee
zupper table?"
Hersch said, "Sometimes they discuss the space
program. One time the topic was the Common Market."
"Vell vat kint of bizness iss zat?" I asked again.
"Mr. and Mrs. Jacobs are very intelligent, you
know," he answered. "She used to be a schoolteacher.
They always have a dinner topic. I find it *stimulating*."
That's when I knew that I had lost Hersch.

The next night at our supper at home I said,
"What do you think will happen if the Russians get
to the moon first?" My fork fell onto the floor.
Dad answered, "Please pass the herring."
I started to pass the dish when it slipped. Only two
pieces slid to the floor, and I put them in the garbage
and immediately wiped the spot with a sponge as I
had always been taught to do.
"Well," I repeated, "What do you think will happen if the Russians get to the moon first?"
Mother said, "Save some of the potatoes for Spencer; he said that he'd be late home."
I helped myself to potatoes; they were buttered
and parsleyed and only one slipped off the dish. I put
it on my plate after I picked it up. I reached for a

roll and knocked over my milk. "Now about the moon," I persisted as I was cupping my hands to catch the dripping and as Mother was running for some paper towels.

Dad looked up and said, "Mark, why don't you try eating on the floor and see if you can drop things up to the table?"

I had to laugh, and so did Mother. There went the space program, Africa, and the Common Market. I never tried to stimulate my family after that. Or Mrs. Jacobs either. Of course, the night that they made the posters for the tryouts was the first time I had seen her since that Friday night supper—*dinner*.

4

IMMEDIATELY AFTER THE NINE AND TEN-YEAR-OLD tryouts, Spencer and Mother had a long kitchen conference. I did my homework in the el so that I could hear. It seems that our town, Point Baldwin, used the auction system. Every guy who isn't a holdover from last year is given a price. Not in money, but in credits. Mother's team, the B'nai B'rith, would have 12,200 credits, which sounded like a million. Except that since Mother had only seven holdovers and except that the B'nai B'rith had finished at the bottom of the league last year and except that she would need a lot of talent. Eight real talented guys to be exact. Good players go for thousands and thousands.

As soon as a manager runs out of credits, he has to

stop bidding on players and wait for the other managers to run out of credits, too. Then everyone finishes filling out his roster from the leftovers. Leftovers play on the team just like anybody else. Nobody is supposed to know whether he was bought or whether he was a leftover. Some guys never know. Some guys can play a whole season and figure that they were paid for just like anybody else. If my mother had not been made manager, I never would have known that I had been one. My mother would not have known it either. Finding out that I was a leftover was the first fringe benefit I got; that is, it was about as much of a one as the night of the tomato soup had been.

I think that we could have lived happily the rest of our lives and not known that I had been bought for free my first year. Hersch, too.

But we wouldn't be free again. It's try now, pay later with the leftovers. The price that Mother would have to pay for us was called an option price and was set by taking an average of what all the managers thought the guy was worth at the end of the year before. The manager that had put up with the guy for a whole season got first dibs on him by saying *yes* he'd pay the option price. If the manager didn't want to pay, the guy would get put up for auction.

Mother would want Hersch and me back, I was sure, and she'd have to use up some of her 12,200 credits to buy us. The least amount a player could be sold for is five hundred credits. I calculated that Hersch and I would cost at least a thousand apiece. At least.

Spencer did most of the talking that night. After he had seen the nine and ten-year-olds, he told Mother that as far as he could see, they would use the minimum number in that age group, which meant that they would take only two. Considering the amount of skill displayed that afternoon, he said that he couldn't see spending a lot for any of those kids.

"We'll take three," Mother said.

"We only have to have two," Spencer reminded her.

"We have to have three; I promised their mothers."

"For crying out loud, Bessie. This is not a wedding invitation list. This is baseball. Do you want a winning team, or don't you?"

"Sure I want a winning team. But we'll take three: Sidney Polsky, Harry Abrams, and Louis LaRosa. I promised their mothers."

"Sidney Polsky? Sidney Polsky! He doesn't have enough coordination to zip his pants. He's a loser, Bessie. We can't have him."

"I tell you, I promised his mother. She called me up special and said that poor Sidney never makes any team, and would I please take him? I figure we can get him cheap. Five hundred credits. That's the minimum. We'll still have 11,700 to splurge with."

"Mother, you can't do that. You can not. Even if you could get him for one hundred fifty, he'll end up being the most expensive player you have. He'll cost you every game because we won't have what we should have had instead of him. He's a *klutz*. He can't field, hit, or pitch. He'll be benched every game. Now think how that will make him feel. He's definitely for the minors. There he'll get some training."

"Spencer darling, what can I tell his mother?"

"You tell his mother to let him make something on his own instead of making phone calls for him. Also tell her to quit driving him everywhere so that he can walk off some of that fat. Then maybe, just maybe, he can run to catch a ball."

"You're right, Spencer, but what shall I tell his mother?"

"I just told you what to tell her."

"Oh, I can't tell her that. She'd never believe me."

"Then tell her anything you want, but I won't have that kid on our team. He's a cry baby, and he doesn't even try."

I yelled in, "They call him the Big Whine."

Mother called back, "Mark, do your homework."

Spencer added his two cents, "Listen, kid, butt out. This is grown-up talk."

I didn't say anything else, but that didn't stop me from thinking anything else. Like if Spencer was so sure he was a grown-up, then he wouldn't have to make remarks reminding me of it.

"Spencer," Mother said, "I see where I'm going to make enemies."

"Not if you handle it well. Just tell Mrs. Polsky what I told you. Only tell it gently."

Then Mother said, "Can I still have Harry and Louis?"

That was disgusting! My mother asking her son, my brother, for permission. Like a kid in school asking for the pass to go to the boys' room. Girls' room.

Spencer replied, "Harry and Louis aren't so bad, and since we have to have two in that age group, they'll do. Provided we can get them for five hundred each."

Mother breathed a sigh of relief. "Thank goodness. I just couldn't tell Mrs. LaRosa 'no.' She's a widow, you know."

Spencer continued with the business of the evening. "Now, tomorrow, when the bigger boys try out, we must look for a good pitcher and at least one strong batter. We'll drop a wad for a good pitcher."

I went to watch the eleven and twelve-year-old tryouts. I knew I didn't have to try out. I felt very in, but I don't think I acted it. Barry Jacobs and Hersch came to watch, too. They kept close to each other, and at first, I stayed with them. But we were like two fingers and a thumb, me being the thumb, a bit shorter and fatter and separated. If I saw them confer together, I wondered if they were joking about me. Wondering about myself was something I had been doing a lot of. Losing your best friend sure takes all the exclamation points out of a guy.

All the managers and coaches of our league were there. Spencer and Mother, like all the others, went around and made notes on a clipboard. Spencer knew what he was doing just as Mother had known what she was doing when she forced him into being coach. Spencer had been catcher on his Little League team. Give him any chance at all, and he'd tell you what a terrific team they had had when he was a youth. That's how he'd refer to that time: "When I was a youth," he'd say. But you had to admit that in his year the B'nai B'rith team had won the championship of our league. And you had to admit that Spencer had been picked as a Tournament player. You had to admit it; it's in the records. Spencer had been catcher in the game that won the district championship for Point Baldwin.

Each team in the Point Baldwin League would pick their best eleven and twelve-year-olds to be on the Tournament Team. Only fourteen guys get chosen from the eight teams. Like All Stars. Our Point Baldwin Tournament Team would play the next town, Rye. If they won that, they would play for area championship, then district, section, state, division, on up to regional champs. Spence's team had lost out at the sectional play-offs. Region champs play

in a World Series of Little League, and that's a big deal. Really big. Little League Baseball, Inc., pays your way to Williamsport, Pennsylvania where the World Series is held. Williamsport, Pennsylvania, is the Jerusalem of Little League.

I figured that with Spencer having already made the tracks, it wouldn't be hard to follow in his footsteps. I began to follow him and his clipboard until he noticed. "What are you doing, kid?"

"Oh, I just thought I'd follow you around, you being my big brother and coach and all."

"Now, listen, kid, don't get mushy. Get unattached. Go pick up somebody your own age."

"There's no one around here I want to play with."

"Hersch is right over there, and so is Barry Jacobs."

"Hersch who?"

"Herschel Dmitri Ivanovich Castro."

"You mean Herschel Miller?"

"Very good. Verrry good. You guessed. Now go. I'm your coach. Not your nursemaid."

"You're also my brother."

"I told you, don't get mushy. Now scat."

That remark was the beginning of the kind of special attention I got the whole season from my brother, my coach.

There had been about sixty boys trying out. When we got home, I sneaked a look at Mother's and Spencer's clipboards. Each boy was listed with his age in parenthesis beside. I came across two names that were underlined and double-starred. On both clipboards.

**Rivera, Simon (11)

**Rivera, Sylvester (11)

There weren't any remarks by their names; there didn't have to be. Those guys were terrific. Identical twins. They had moved to Point Baldwin from Miami in September. Any team would be lucky to get one, but they would be auctioned as a package. The League didn't like to break up manager and son or brother and brother. Franklin P. Botts was also underlined. A powerful batter. He had only one star and one underline; the Chicken Delights had given up his option.

Spencer and Mother now had to draw up a list of the players they wanted in order of preference. I didn't even look at that list. I had my own idea about where I stood, and I didn't want to know if I was exactly right. I was relieved when Mother sent me to bed.

Spencer had to study for some exam the night of the auction, so Mother went without him. You wouldn't believe the list of instructions he gave her. And she listened! You would think that he was a candidate for King of England, and my mother acted as if no one had ever taught her that kings get born not elected.

She returned home about 10:30 and called to Spencer and Dad right away. "We got them. We got them. The twins, we got. Cost me 6,800 credits for the two, but we got them. Also picked up Botts. Cheap for him, only 1975. What do you suppose is wrong with him that he was so cheap?"

Spencer then asked about some of the others, and they talked on about how she couldn't get Romano because she ran out of credits, so she just picked up her nine and ten-year-olds for five hundred each and came home.

Spencer must have been looking over the list when he saw my name. "What! You spent nine hundred and twenty-five credits for Mark. Nine hundred and twenty-five? You could have gotten him for eight hundred. That was his option price. Didn't you pick up his option? He should have cost only eight hundred."

Mother answered, "Yes, by the way, how is my Moshe?"

By the way, how is he? That's the first that she had asked about me. I was less than a hobby to her.

"He's fine," Spencer said, but he wasn't willing to stop his accounting. He must have inherited a counting gene from Dad.

"How come he cost you nine hundred twenty-five credits? Tell me, Bessie, didn't you pick up his option?"

"Well," Mother said, "I let his option go and put

him up for auction. I pushed the bidding up to nine hundred twenty-five. I figured that no son of mine would go for only eight hundred. Especially when Hersch's option was a thousand."

"Hersch happens to be a better batter than your son."

"But he's not nearly as cute."

"Bessie Setzer! You can't run a team on heart."

"Yes, you can. If you've got guts, too." Long pause. Then Mother said very quietly, "By the way, I bought Sidney Polsky. I couldn't tell his mother what you told me to tell her."

"Mother! You're impossible. No wonder you couldn't afford Romano. I let you out of my sight for one evening, and you . . ."

I didn't listen any more even though they were talking loud enough for good eavesdropping. I was worth only eight hundred, and I was experienced. Finding out that I was only one and three fifths as good as Sidney Polsky was about as joyful news as finding out that I had been a leftover. Only it was worse. Having everyone in your family know your option price makes you feel like you have nothing on in front of them. Nothing but a big tattoo saying 800.

Hersch, who didn't even care about baseball nearly as much as I did, was worth twice as much as Sidney. I was a cheap outfielder. Only eight hundred credits. The one hundred twenty-five was sales tax just because I'm Moshe, my mother's son. No one was allowed to tell auction prices. The other kids who were cheap would never know it. If I hadn't been trying to outgrow the habit, I would have cried.

I would never let my manager and my coach know that I had listened in. I would just be nonchalant about the whole thing, but I would be terrific, simply terrific on the field.

5

THE ORTHODONTIST TIGHTENED MY BRACES LATE ON
the Saturday before our first practice. On Sunday I
was in pain. But pain. About seven out of ten kids in
my Hebrew Class wore braces. When the class
laughed, it looked like an open face mine with a silver
lode one third of the way down. You could tell when
someone got theirs tightened; their noses would be
pink and their eyes watery: like before Dristan.

Aunt Thelma and Uncle Ben came to dinner on
Sunday. Aunt Thelma had a habit of rapidly becoming an expert on anything Mother got involved in.
Like the herb garden. That is, in addition to being an
expert in her two specialties: raising other people's
children and educating them. Aunt Thelma has one

49

maid, Valerie, and one husband, Uncle Ben. Both the maid and Uncle Ben commute to work. And even if she had kids, I don't know why Mother should listen because Aunt Thelma is the *younger* sister, even if she is richer. But Aunt Thelma went to daytime college and finished. Mother went to nighttime college, part-time, and quit when she met Dad who was also going to nighttime college, part-time. They still talk about how Mom worked so that Dad could go to daytime college, full-time, and finish being an accountant. They talk about it often. You'd think that they'd have gotten over it by now. I figured that my mother respected education, and that's why she put up with Aunt Thelma. Spencer, also.

Although Mother didn't like to have both hostessing and baseball on her mind at the same time, she put out a nice meal. Pot roast and cheese cake. Mother is great with cheese cake; she tops it with strawberries.

Aunt Thelma was dieting; dieting is part of Aunt Thelma's character. Dieters annoy Mother. When she was pot roasting and cheese caking, she expected everyone to eat a lot. Because of the braces I let her down, too.

Mother commented as she was clearing up, "I'm putting away more than I put out." She always said that when we had company.

Aunt Thelma and I made an effort to help Mother clean up, but when Mother is aggravated, she is very difficult to help. Like when I asked, "Where should I put the leftover roast?" Mother didn't answer. She sighed, wiped her hands on her apron, and took it from me. Looking straight at me, she wrapped it in aluminum foil, and then with movements like a ballet dancer, put it in the refrigerator. As she closed the refrig, she said, "I started keeping leftover roast in a refrigerator five minutes after it got invented." Aunt Thelma never looked comfortable in a kitchen; she perspired. And I wasn't comfortable; my whole face felt on the verge of pain except when I chewed, and then it felt in actual pain.

By the time we arrived at the practice field, Mother was exhausted, and Spencer was irritated. Dad had decided to stay home and read; he always went on a reading jag after tax season. Uncle Ben chose to keep him company. As soon as we got there, Aunt Thelma ran out onto the field full of dignified enthusiasm until her heels sank into the ground and she began tilting backwards. After that she sat on the bench and observed.

The team arrived in dribs and drabs after we did. They came in carloads driven by mothers who were all dressed like Aunt Thelma in stretch pants and ski jackets with their hair all pasted together. The trouble with the way Aunt Thelma looked was that when she walked, nothing moved but her legs. When Mother walks, it's like she carries a private breeze with her, and that's much nicer.

Mother herded all the kids into the dugout and

began by introducing herself and Spencer. "My name is Mrs. Setzer. Here is Spencer who is your coach." There was dead silence. Mother smiled and cleared her throat, "I'm your manager."

There followed one loud snort from the left end of the dugout. Mother ignored it and continued, "I think we can be a winning team if you listen to me and to Spencer and work hard and train hard." The snort was louder and longer this time. Mother ignored it again. "After this we'll practice every Tuesday afternoon and Friday before sundown unless there is rain." Again the snort. Everyone began to laugh. Mother cocked her ear this time and listened, "Would you please repeat that?" she requested. Her head remained tilted, but she kept her eyes from the left side of the dugout. There followed a double snort. Everyone laughed again. Louder. "Does someone here have trouble with adenoids?" she asked. Spencer was getting nervous; he began picking imaginary lint off his pants, a sure sign that he was nervous.

Hal Burser pointed to Botts and said, "Botts wants to know why we have to have a lady manager. Like why can't we have a man?"

"If Botts wants to know, let Botts ask," Mother said.

Botts asked. "Why do we have to have a lady manager?" His voice kind of trailed off at the end of the question.

Mother said, "The question has been asked and seconded, 'Why do we have to have a lady manager?' There is only one possible explanation." She paused, took a deep breath, and with her hands straight down at her sides, said, "The reason why you have a lady manager is because chlorophyll is a catalyst that enables a plant to use the energy of the sun to convert carbon dioxide and water into sugar and oxygen."

Long, long pause. No snorts. Nothing. We all waited, but Mother said nothing more. She just folded her arms across her chest and tapped her foot and smiled at the whole dugout, her audience. We were all puzzled.

Finally, Hersch said, "But, Mrs. Setzer, that about chlorophyll is just a fact of life."

Mother didn't give his sentence a chance to cool off before she pressed in hers, "And so is your having a lady manager! It's just a fact of life, and you have to face it. You have to face facts." Then she took her arms from her chest and raised them outward. She shrugged her shoulders and smiled at the boys. "Now that we have that over with, can we play ball?"

Spencer laughed first. I was second. We gave everyone the cue that it was all right to laugh, and they did. When the laughter died down, naturally died down, I started it again by making out that I had an uncontrollable urge that I tried to stifle behind my hand. Finally, the second laughter died, too. It wasn't as long or as hard as the first. I wasn't tempted to start it again because I caught a certain look from Spencer.

Sidney Polsky raised his hand and said, "Mrs. Setzer, would you mind repeating that so that I can tell my mother?"

Mother responded, "All right, you guys, now when someone, anyone, asks you why you have a lady manager, you tell them. Now repeat after me: The reason why you have a lady manager is because chlorophyll is a catalyst . . ."

And we all repeated after Mother; that was our first lesson in baseball that season. As the kids left the dugout for the playing field, they chanted it to themselves. After the last of the team was on the field I saw Mother look up to where the light fixture should have been but there was only sky, and I heard her mutter, "That was a good idea about the chlorophyll. Left over from the herb garden, but good." She kissed the tips of one set of fingers and then the other and held them upward for the breeze to send those kisses to the Deity who had moved with her to the ball park.

After those introductions, we began calisthenics; every time I leaned down to touch my toes, I felt rivers of pain leap up in my head. And when we ran around the bases to loosen up, the vibrations set my whole head to quaking each time I put my foot down. After doing awful two times at bat, I retired. Spencer was pitching batting practice, and he could have fed them to me a bit softer. He being my brother and all. Besides, he knew about the braces. As I walked to the bench, I said to myself, "Think of Sandy Koufax." And then I answered myself, "Sandy Koufax had a much more dramatic ailment than just crooked teeth. Great pains make great heroes, but toothaches just make lousy batting averages." So I sat out and watched.

The twins were terrific. They were like two pros among us. Simon and Sylvester looked as if they were looking in a mirror when they faced each other. Completely identical except that one was right-handed and the other was a lefty. They parted their hair on opposite sides, too. There's a word for twins like that; they're called mirror-image twins. They were both great at pitching as well as batting. But if you're looking at narrow differences, the lefty was a little bit better. A tiny bit. Not enough to hurt the other's feelings. Both of them were good-natured and kind to the other kids.

Barry Jacobs was also good at batting, but he wasn't so kind to other kids. I guess it's easier to be kind when you're as superior as Simon and Sylvester than when you're just working-at-it good like Barry. Simon and Sylvester giving out smiles and helpful hints to the others was like a gift from the Ford Foundation; there was still lots there, and they didn't do it for profit.

Aunt Thelma helped measure the boys for uniforms, and I helped give them out. Sidney cried when he found out that he wouldn't have his baseball pants right away. His mother mentioned to Aunt Thelma that he was a little overweight. Actually, Sidney was fat. His pants would have to be ordered. Sidney was wiping the tears from his eyes with his fists the way that infants do, when his mother came swooping down onto the field looking like a jagged streak of yellow lightning in her yellow stretch pants with knees going at forty-five degree angles.

Mother was standing behind Hersch telling him to choke up a bit more on the bat.

"Mrs. Setzer," Mrs. Polsky began.

Mother waved a hand impatiently. She wanted to finish with Hersch.

"Mrs. Setzer," Mrs. Polsky repeated.

Mother finished with Hersch and then said, "Yes, Mrs. Polsky?"

"Isn't there some way Sidney can get into a pair of pants?"

Mother glanced from Mrs. Polsky to Sidney and then back again. "Sure," she said, "tell him to lose about ten pounds." She looked over at Sidney again and added, "Around the hips would be best."

Spencer came over and added that he had a new training rule: all the boys were to walk to practice and to the games. They all needed the leg work.

Mrs. Polsky sputtered, "But my Sidney doesn't get home until 3:15. By the time he gets a little snack and changes his clothes, how can he have time to walk to practice?"

Spencer thought a minute and answered, "He can skip his snack and ride his bike."

Mother looked at Spencer and said, "That's a great idea, Spence."

Sidney tugged at his mother's slacks and said, "Can I, Mom? Can I?"

Mrs. Polsky answered, "I'll have to think about it, son."

Aunt Thelma chimed in, "I think, Mrs. Polsky, that it would be a very good experience for Sidney to ride his bike to the games."

Mother said, "What's this about a good experience? It's a training rule; Spencer just said so."

Sidney kept asking, "Can I? Can I?" and Mrs. Polsky kept saying, "We'll see. We'll see." She glared at Mother quite a lot.

After calisthenics and measuring for uniforms, we had a practice game. It was hardly that, though. Sidney was in right field, and the only time that a ball came his way was when Sylvester hit one. Sidney was scratching at the time, and Sylvester ran all the bases. Other things like that happened, too. For example, Barry hit a low grounder on which he easily made it to second because the ball kept rolling out of the first baseman's hand. I happened to be playing first base at the time. When I finally got enough hand on the ball, Barry had just rounded second. I threw it to Louis LaRosa on third. He caught it surprisingly enough—the first, firm catch of the afternoon. But when he caught it, he was so pleased with himself that he stepped off base to look around and see if his mother was watching (she was), and he neglected to tag Barry out. Barry made it to home even before the throw.

Spencer continued not giving me any special breaks. He kept referring to himself as *let's* and to me as *kid*. "Let's beef up that swing, kid." "Let's run as if it counts, kid." "Let's get that bat off your shoulder, kid."

Mother said, "That's all for today, boys." As they were leaving the field, she addressed You-Know-Who and said, "For all of Egypt You sent down ten plagues. For me, Bessie Setzer, you send just one. Frogs. A whole field of leap frogs. I tell You, Lord, one is enough." I could see Mother calculating that she had one month of hard work to whip our team into shape. Only Mother wouldn't whip; she'd nag, and rage and coax.

Spencer threw all the equipment into the back seat and sat in front next to Mother. That would have left Aunt Thelma and me as roommates in the back seat. Except that Aunt Thelma never took a back seat to anyone, and she crowded up front with Mother and Spence.

I leaned over the front seat and asked my brother, my coach, "How did I do?"

He said, "You act as if you're afraid of the ball, kid."

We had all of six players out of fifteen who didn't act afraid of the ball. Maybe I was afraid because I was conscious of the fact that if the ball hit anywhere near my mouth, I'd be swallowing about $950.00 worth of braces and fillings. I don't know what reasons the others had.

I decided not to mention my reasons. Instead I asked, "How do you become unafraid?"

"Mostly by becoming more sure of yourself," he answered.

That's like telling a poor man he would stop being poor if he had more money! I figured that I didn't even have to answer Spencer, my brother, my coach, if that was the way he was going to be bighearted about giving me advice.

As we came back into the house, I realized that my mouth had stopped hurting. "What's to eat?" I yelled.

Mother let loose. "What's to eat? What's to eat? Now you ask what's to eat! What's the matter, your stomach can't run on Eastern Daylight Savings Time? Right now, putting away all the equipment and washing up. That's to eat."

Aunt Thelma left for home even before our car was emptied. She almost forgot Uncle Ben.

We had leftover pot roast. I shouldn't have asked.

6

BEING NONCHALANT AND GETTING YOUR BRACES tightened don't make you terrific on the field. You have to practice in between regular times. So the Saturday after our first two team practices I skipped Sabbath services at the synagogue. It was an easy caper, men. I dressed as usual in my good clothes befitting the Sabbath. I left the house, hair parted and combed. On the way out of my residence, I deposited my prayer book and prayer cap in the mailbox, and at the same time I removed my mitt and sneakers from the mailbox. I had wisely deposited mitt and sneakers in the mailbox the night before. Calculating that Sabbath services are normally over at 11:00, I thought that I could return to my house by 11:15, a safe half hour before the mail would be delivered.

As soon as I left the house, I began walking in the direction of my family's house of worship, known as the synagogue, but I circled back and walked toward Water Street downtown. I successfully avoided detection and arrived at three large brick buildings erected by the U.S. Government.

Five years ago when they were being built, a huge sign in front of the buildings had said that they were LOW INCOME HOUSING. And that's what they had been called before anyone moved into them. Now everyone called them the projects. Two of the buildings faced each other but not the street, and the tallest faced the street but not the other two. All were set well back from the sidewalk, and all the land in front of and around them was done to in one way or another. Patches of grass and walks and a small playground with swings whose seats were low and made of tough leather, which was probably some kind of plastic. Steel mesh wastepaper baskets were chained to trees. There was also a part surrounded by a Cyclone steel fence, which was surrounded by shrubs. That was where the voices came from.

I walked over. The gate was open. There were four undressed basketball hoops, two at each end, but the shouts were baseball shouts. I knew there would be a baseball game there. Botts and the twins had talked about it at practice the day before, and I had listened in. I hoped they would let me in and that if they did,

I could play and be lousy and not have to worry about being lousy. When a guy's mother manages and his brother coaches, a guy feels that he loses his right to be awful. A guy feels like he's Exhibit A. Permanent Exhibit A. In Gimbels' downtown window. I spotted Simon and Sylvester and cautiously waved hi.

One twin yelled to the other, "Hey, look who's here."

I loosened my tie and waited over by the gate. One twin approached and said, "You can play as soon as we get one more kid to even up the teams. I always make an even number." He looked me over, and at first said nothing about the way I was dressed, but I could tell that he was thinking it. Finally, he pointed to my sneaks and said, "Why don't you put those on while you're waiting."

Fortune walked in a few minutes later. Fortune was Simon and Sylvester's twelve-year-old sister, whom everyone called Cookie. She wore cut-off blue jeans and was small. Small-boned, you'd call it, I guess. It was as if Simon and Sylvester were the originals and Cookie was a model of them—like those miniature statues of Venus or The Thinker that you see in bookstores. Her hair was medium long, and the blunt bottom ends stuck out. Her eyes were as black as but bigger than Simon's and Sylvester's. That is, when you could see them. Her hair covered them as well as her ears. When she pushed her hair back, you could see that her ears were rather large and had tiny gold earrings going through small holes in the lobe part. Also her mouth was too big for her face. But she acted as if she was beautiful. She was.

She walked with one hand on her hip over to one twin and said, "I'll take your team today."

The other one yelled, "O.K., Setzer, I've got you. Take third."

No introductions. No directions. I didn't even know where third was. I casually draped my jacket over the fence, to show that I was not cold and that I was ready. I put on my mitt and looked around. Casually.

Cookie glanced at me and then pointed to a faint chalk mark on the blacktop. I mounted my base. Fortune swung and missed three times before leaving the plate. That was the third out for that side, and she acted so nonchalant, looking down at her nails and pulling a piece of cuticle. She sighed and walked to first base, hands on hips, one leg slightly in front of the other, pointed elbows in back. In profile she looked like a pointy capital R.

I was shocked. From the way she had acted and knowing whose sister she was, and considering the fact that she was a girl, and that they still let her play, I had expected her to be great. She wasn't even good, and they had let her in so easily.

Simon pitched to me next; I saw the ball would be low, so I let it pass. "Ball one," I called. No argument. They knew it was a ball. I took the next pitch, swung and missed, but I connected on the third. I looked around to see if everyone was ready to admire me, but they acted about the same as they did when Cookie struck out. And that was the main thing I liked about playing at the Projects; no one performed . . . everyone just played and tried to win. Sylvester followed me; he took the first pitch and hit the ball close to the fence, but the kid on third who looked at least fourteen years old, having the beginnings of a beard and all, caught it with one hand scraping the fence. It went that way all the time. Their fielding was terrific. Even Fortune was good at that.

"How come you guys never miss a ball?" I asked.

"Necessity," laughed the kid with the beginnings of a beard.

Sylvester explained. "Windows."

They all laughed together. Then the twin continued, "Windows means no hard balls allowed. The super has a fit when he finds us using one, but he don't find out unless we miss and break a window. So we see to it that he don't find out. Ever. We don't miss. Ever."

I wished I had never asked. The thought of missing made me nervous. "Why don't you guys use a soft ball then? That'd be playing it safe. That's what you should do."

"We can't afford to do that. The minute we use a soft ball, the fielding gets sloppy."

"I get it," I said and smiled. But it wasn't exactly a smile of relief.

Playgirl finally broke up the game. *Playgirl* being the magazine that Franklin P. Botts carried under his arm when he arrived and stood waiting by the fence. The kids crowded around him, and he collected a nickel from each of them. I didn't have any money with me; you're not supposed to take money to synagogue on Sabbath. I stretched my head to see if I could get a peek at the fold-out center picture. I knew what she wasn't wearing, but I couldn't get close enough to see anything important. I guess Cookie didn't have any money either.

She told me, "Botts went to camp. Overnight camp. Some rich relative, an aunt or something, sent him. When he came back, he taught us four dirty songs and started buying *Playgirl*. His Little League coach benched him four games last year, one for each song. And this year that coach didn't bother to pick up his option. But Botts doesn't care as long as he gets his price. He always charges admission. Some of the kids buy so many looks that they could have bought the magazine in the first place, but I guess they're always afraid to bring it into the house."

"Oh, I'd take a look if I had the money. But you can't take money to synagogue on Sabbath. Synagogue!" I yelled. "What time is it?" No answer. "What time is it? Somebody, what time is it? Somebody? Anybody?"

Botts yelled back, "It's five after eleven." He had a watch.

"Oh, boy. Oh, boy," I muttered as I grabbed my jacket off the fence. The prongs tore the lining a little. "Oh, boy," I said again as I began to make a dash for it. I had meant to ask the time when I arrived so that I could gauge how long the return trip would take, but I had gotten involved and forgot all about it.

Cookie ran after me carrying my shoes. "What's the matter?" she called, "you turn into a pumpkin or something at five after eleven?"

Botts laughed. "No, a bagel!" Everyone else laughed, too, although I'd bet that half of them didn't know what a bagel was.

"His ma's the manager of our team, the B'nai Bagels," he said, laughing. Getting up from the center of his group, he yelled to me, "What does *b'nai* mean, anyway?"

I answered, walking backwards so they could hear me, but so that I wouldn't lose more time getting home. "*Sons of*. It means *sons of* in Hebrew."

"Then we're all Sons of Bagels?" one of the twins asked, smiling to his brother.

Cookie was still running alongside me; she kept tossing that hair out of her eyes. "What's a bagel?"

"What I'll turn into in about ten minutes." I turned around and began running sincerely.

I arrived home before the mail and stashed my

shoes and mitt in the shrubbery in front of the house to retrieve later. Aunt Thelma's car was in the driveway. I don't know why she even has a convertible because she doesn't like her hair to blow. She must like to put the top down to air out the upholstery.

They were having coffee at the kitchen table when I walked in. The dining room table was covered rim to rim with the records of last season's games: Mom's homework.

"How were services?" Mom asked.

"The usual," I answered. I glanced up at the light fixture before hurrying upstairs to hang up my jacket before the lining got discovered.

"Why," Aunt Thelma asked as I got to the stairs, "do you allow that boy to wear tennis shoes to Sabbath services?"

I was grateful that I was upstairs and out of sight.

"Allow? I don't allow," Mother answered. "He just wore them. Better that he should wear sneakers to synagogue on Saturday morning, Thelma, than that he shouldn't go at all. I'm sure the dear Lord wouldn't care if he walked in unshoed."

"Unshod," Aunt Thelma corrected.

"Shod? I thought horses get shod."

"Shod is the past tense of shoe," Aunt Thelma informed.

"I'm sure the dear Lord wouldn't care if he walked in BAREFOOTED," Mother said.

Aunt Thelma sniffed.

I rejoined the family downstairs just as Dad walked in. He started taking off his tie the minute he crossed the threshold. He always did. Dad didn't have office hours on Saturday; it just seemed that way. He always had to catch up. I guess homework is a way of life for some people. Only they call book bags briefcases when they get older. Truth was, my dad really likes books. He would rather read about a baseball game than see one. That's a fact. He read the sports page as thoroughly as the international news, but I never saw him throw a ball or watch a game on TV. He wandered toward the dining room table as he was loosening his tie.

"What's all this, Bessie?" he asked.

Mother called back from the kitchen, "Last year's Little League records, Sam. I thought they would help, but they're not too much use. There are so many new players this year."

Dad began looking over the records, and Aunt Thelma emerged from the kitchen holding her saucer chest high in the palm of one hand and her coffee cup with the thumb and forefinger of the other; her head would dart down now and then, and she'd sip from the cup in a motion that looked like a duck straining water.

Besides books, my Dad's good at concentrating.

Aunt Thelma sipped again and said, "Hello, Samuel." Aunt Thelma was the only person who called my father *Samuel* and my mother *Bess*. Even

Spencer called Mother *Bessie,* and he wasn't supposed to.

Dad's head darted up. "Oh, hi, Thelma. How is Ben?"

"Ben has a head cold."

Mother erupted from the kitchen before Dad had a chance to answer. "Men with such a little bit of hair should wear hats."

"What do you mean?" Aunt Thelma asked. "It's been at least seventy-five degrees out for the past week. Why should Ben wear a hat?"

"Because," Mother continued, "your Ben is practically—you should excuse the expression—practically bald. And when he perspires, his scalp gets wet and then the slightest breeze and he's holding open house for viruses."

"Science has found that there is no relationship between getting a chill and getting a cold."

"That's what science has found out for this week, Thelma, but wait five minutes. They'll find out what our mother always said. That men who are absolutely bald like Ben should wear hats."

Aunt Thelma sniffed.

Dad continued glancing over the records. He did it very fast, numbers sort of being his business. "It seems that the total in the errors column is extraordinarily high," he said.

"Well, after all," Mother said, " This is Little League. We're not the L.A. Dodgers, you know. Or even the

New York Mets."

"Now, Bessie, don't get offended. I'm just doing an account analysis. My recommendation to you is to win by cutting down on the errors. Concentrate on your defense for the first part of the season. It doesn't appear that the other teams have such great batters. And at the beginning of the season, most of the hits were made on errors. Practically every run the Elks Club team made against the B'nai B'rith was a home run. That means a lot of monkey business in the outfield. Errors. My advice to you, Bessie, is to cut your losses by tightening up on defense. Follow that up with batting."

Mother gave Dad a big kiss. "Sam, you are a genius."

"I know, Bessie, I know," Dad answered, looking at Aunt Thelma from under his eyebrows. He was pleased about himself and embarrassed about Aunt Thelma. When Mom was happy with someone, her enthusiasm was awful. You can't avoid it or even help catching it.

"You see, Thelma, my Sam not only has something *on* his head: hair, but something *in* his head: brains."

"My Ben is no slouch in the brains department, either," Aunt Thelma answered.

"That's true," Mother said. "Ben *is* bright even if he's as bald as a baby's backside."

Aunt Thelma took long enough to set her cup and saucer on top of last year's records before she marched out of the house.

Mother looked at Dad and said, "What ever did I say wrong, Sam?"

Dad shook his head at Mother and ran after Aunt Thelma, who couldn't get her car out of our driveway because ours was blocking hers. Dad brought her back.

"I demand an apology," she hissed at Mother.

"O.K. An apology. I'm sorry that Ben is bald."

Aunt Thelma threw up her arms and began marching out of the house again. Dad caught her by the shoulders and turned her around. The two sisters faced each other and glared. The air between them growled.

And Aunt Thelma charged, "Good grief, Bess! I want you to be sorry for hurting my feelings, not for Ben's being bald."

"Did I hurt your feelings? I didn't realize."

"You didn't realize because you didn't care. All you care about is having a winning team. Ever since you've become manager, that's all you care about. Is that more important than hurting people's feelings?"

"What you don't realize," Mother said, "is what will be hurt if we don't have a winning team."

"Don't be ridiculous. Nothing will be hurt. One of the values of Little League is to teach the boys to win and lose gracefully."

"Except how can a team learn to win and lose gracefully when all they do is lose? Then they lose something else, too. Their fight they lose; that's where the hurt comes in. Their spirit gets hurt. I saw it in my own Mark here. At the end of last season he never felt it mattered whether his team even showed up at the ball park. They forgot how to care. I want to do something much harder than teaching them how to win and lose gracefully. I want to teach them to care. I want they should feel rotten when they lose."

"You want them to feel rotten?" Aunt Thelma repeated.

Mother nodded. "Rotten but not hopeless."

"If you take Samuel's advice, you're going to make them specialists. Offense. Defense. Sounds like platoons in professional football. And you can't tell me that's good for Little League."

"Strategy that is. Training. Discipline. They need that to make caring count. It would be mean to make them care, and then not give them the training to make caring count."

Aunt Thelma sucked in her breath and added, "I'm not convinced that . . ."

I interrupted Aunt Thelma in a voice that belonged out-of-doors, "You can't accuse my mother of being interested only in winning. That's not true, and I can prove it in two words. Just two words!"

Aunt Thelma, Mother and Dad all focused on me. I backed up to the wall in the el, swallowed, and whispered, "Sidney Polsky."

Dad laughed. "The case for the defense rests." The sisters laughed, too, and it was a good thing. It turned out that we needed Aunt Thelma on our side. And I was surprised at how quickly I had come to my mother's defense, even though I didn't approve of her language. (I would have bet that Mrs. Jacobs never even *thought* that anyone was as bald as a baby's backside.) It seems I had no trouble with my mother, the mother; it was my mother, the manager, who gave me headaches and doubts.

7

EIGHT DAYS LATER I DISCOVERED THAT IT WASN'T
Spencer, my brother, who wouldn't give me any
good advice; it was just Spencer, my coach, who
wouldn't. Spencer, my brother, helped me with a
difficult personal problem. He actually taught me
something.

To begin with I don't believe that you should try
to teach an animal something that is completely un-
natural to that animal. Like I always feel uncomfortable when I see poodles walking on two legs on the
Ed Sullivan Show. I don't feel so bad when they heel
and sit and obey commands because, after all, everyone likes a chance to show off about how smart he is.
But when dogs walk on two legs, I feel the strain.

Personally. It's not natural. It's not natural either for me to sing. I am a born listener, and even that I don't do too well since I was born with low fi ears, equipment which is very hard on a Jewish boy about to become Bar Mitzvah. Because it happens that a very important part of your Bar Mitzvah training involves learning to chant—which is next door to singing.

For a normal Bar Mitzvah you have to do these things, solo, in public. The rabbi at our synagogue makes a tape recording of your section of the reading, the *haftorah* it's called, and they lend you this tape player so that you can hear it and sing-along-with-rabbi. I was to be pitied. It's bad enough not being able to sing, but it's worse not to be able to tell if you're flat. And it's even worse to have a class full of guys who can do both. In public school I always faked it by moving my mouth and having nothing come out, but among other things that that Bar Mitzvah year had brought out in public was my low key, off key voice. Sunday mornings was when we practiced our *haftorahs*. I was considering having mine ghost-sung on tape, but they won't allow you to plug in any electrical appliances in our synagogue on Sabbath. And my Bar Mitzvah would be then. They always are in our synagogue.

That Sunday Barry had done his usual, sterling job, and Rabbi Hershfield had made his usual observation, "If all of you boys try, you can do as well as Benyamin." Benyamin was Barry, who was practically a baritone already. Rabbi Hershfield didn't know about genes, I guess.

Rabbi nodded toward me and said, "Now we'll hear Moshe. Let's begin." Then, as if his eyes suddenly came into focus, he added, "Why did you miss services on Saturday?"

"A virus," I answered. I was surprised at how easily I did that. Lying in Hebrew School. For just a minute I expected the floor to open and me to drop into the school basement if not someplace lower. Nothing happened, and I looked up at one of the light fixtures to say thanks. Boy, the crazy habits a guy can pick up from his mother.

"What about the Saturday before?"

"It was a twenty-four hour virus."

"Once a week from sunset Friday until sunset Saturday? Just like the Sabbath?"

"Just like," I repeated. I felt bad that he believed me so easily. My eyes wandered up toward the light fixture again. I wouldn't have been surprised if it had lighted up and said TILT.

"Do you feel better today?" Rabbi asked.

"Yes, sir."

"Can you sing?" he asked gently.

"Well, sir, neither of us has thought so until now."

Rabbi laughed, and so did the rest of the class. Barry and Hersch included.

"Begin," Rabbi said. He closed his eyes. I think that closed eyes are the mark of a good listener. When

I want to really hear something, I close my eyes and open my mouth. Even for TV. It's not pretty, but it works.

I did my piece, no better and no worse than usual. I sort of whisper-sing. When Rabbi opened his eyes, he looked as if he were going to cry or change his profession.

"You have not been practicing," he accused.

"I've been practicing. In the shower. I sing in the shower."

"In the shower? Why there? Why do you sing in the shower?"

"Because, sir, Niagara Falls is not available."

That got my second laugh for the day. Twice out of Barry, too.

"Moshe," Rabbi said, "you need help. Why don't you ask your brother Schmuel to help you." *Schmuel* is Spencer's Hebrew name, but you better never remind him of it.

"Yes, sir," I answered. But I was thinking that it would take more than my brother's help. It would take divine help. Or a new set of genes. Or both.

Spencer was reading the Sunday *New York Times* when I arrived home. He had his feet—socks on, shoes off—up on the coffee table. And the *Times* was spread around him like a bunch of bed sheets after a bad night. I stood in front of him waiting for him to feel my presence, the way they always do in books. He concentrates very hard, my brother. He didn't seem to feel my presence, so I cracked my knuckles. That worked. He lowered the paper; he needed a shave.

"You rang?" he asked.

"Rabbi said that you could help me with my *haftorah*."

"Memorize. You have to memorize most of it so that it just looks as if you're reading it." He began to lift his paper again.

"I'm not worried about the words. It's the singing. I can't sing."

"No one in our family can."

"But when I sing, it's annoying. It's like the drip of a faucet or the sound of a single fly trapped in the rear window of the car. Annoying. You can't wait for it to stop. How did you get by, Spence?"

"Dad gave me some advice. I'll see if you can use the same advice. First, I have to hear you sing. Sing something."

"Here? Now? In front of you?"

"Here. Now. In front of me."

"What shall I sing?"

"I don't care. Sing anything. Sing *Deep Purple*."

"What's *Deep Purple*? I don't know *Deep Purple*."

"So sing *The Star Spangled Banner*."

"Naw. You'll have to stand up."

"No, I won't. You just have to stand up in public. C'mon now sing. *Oh, say, can you* . . ."

"It's disrespectful not to stand up if someone is

singing our national anthem."

"It is not. You just have to have a respectful *attitude*. That's all you show by standing up. A respectful attitude."

"You sure don't look respectable with your beard on your face and your feet on the table."

"I can feel respect*ful*. And I do, unshaven and unshod as I am."

"I thought horses get shod," I answered.

"Also people," Mother called in from the kitchen. You can hear anything everywhere in that house. "Shod is the past tense of shoe."

"Just checking," I called back.

Spencer's head whipped from me to the kitchen door and back again. "Checking on who—whom?"

"Your Aunt Thelma," Mother called in from the kitchen.

"What's Aunt Thelma got to do with all this?" Spencer asked Mother through the wall.

"So, Moshe, come help set the table, or we'll be late with eating. Your Aunt Thelma comes again! *Da-rum, da-rum, da-rum, dum, dum. Heigh ho! Thelma!*"

I burst into song, "*Oh, say, can you see . . .*"

Mother walked in from the kitchen, and Spencer jumped to his feet, threw one hand over his chest, clutched the paper with the other, and stood in front of me. Mother's eyebrows curled into question marks as she looked at Spencer. Then she moved to attention

right there by the kitchen door and crossed her heart with the hand holding the wooden spoon.

"*What so proudly we hailed . . .*" I continued in my tip-toe alto.

They both stood there until I had finished the whole first stanza. Then Spencer said, "O.K., boy, ready for the good word?"

"I'm ready already. I've been ready," I told Spencer.

"I have only one word of advice to give you."

"Give already."

"That word is *fortissimo.*"

"Thanks a lot. What's *fortissimo*? Italian for shod?"

"No, it's Italian for *loud.* When in doubt, shout. That's what I'm telling you."

"I should shout? Everyone will hear for sure how bad I am."

"But, my dear brother, if you sing loud and clear, it will be easier on the audience. You're making it doubly hard on them. Hard to listen to and hard to hear. Now, let's have another stanza of *The Star Spangled Banner.* FORTISSIMO." And he held up his arms as if he were holding a baton, and he closed his eyes as if he couldn't bear to both see and hear and not because he was being a good listener.

"I only know the first stanza."

He opened his eyes only long enough to clamp his hand over them. That's what Spencer did when he wanted you to know that he was being patient. "O.K. Let's hear that again. Once more. With vigor."

"*Oh, say, can you see by the* . . ." I sang fortissimo. And loved it.

Mother waited until *whose broad stripes and bright stars* before she began applauding. "Fine. Fine," she said. "Now, if we're finished with Ted Mack's Original Amateur Hour, you can come into the kitchen and help me set the table. On the way in you can sign autographs." As I started toward the kitchen, she added, "We must finish the main course or we'll be late for Aunt Thelma."

"Are we having Aunt Thelma for dessert or something?" Spencer asked.

"For dessert your aunt is coming to discuss baseball. She has become very interested. Also she is becoming very informed. She just read Sandy Koufax's autobiography, and she thinks she'll come to practices with us."

"And I just read a book on child care, so I think I'll have a baby."

"Spencer, don't be vulgar." And with that Mother lifted her chin and marched back into the kitchen.

8

THE FOLLOWING SATURDAY I WENT TO THE PROJECTS in the afternoon, and I quietly gave a dollar to Simon; he was supposed to give it to his oldest brother, Julio, who was out of school and working at the Atlantic station. He said that Julio wouldn't mind buying it for me. It only cost seventy-five cents, but I didn't have the exact change. I could have asked Spencer to buy it, but being that Spencer had too much to do with my life already, I didn't want to ask him. The man at the drugstore didn't keep them on the rack with *Better Homes and Gardens* and all the other magazines; you had to look eligible for the draft before he would drag one out from under the counter and sell it to you. We made arrangements for

84

me to pick it up the following day at the Projects.

I could hardly wait to get there. After Sunday School I inhaled my lunch and dashed over. I arrived before anyone else was around. Most of the kids including Botts hadn't finished their lunch after their church. At last one of the twins appeared. I yelled "hi" and then whispered, "Did you bring it?"

The twin said, "Sylvester will."

We sat and talked a little bit while the rest of the kids were coming out of their apartments. One more twin arrived, and they began choosing up sides. I worked my way over to the other twin and said, "Did you bring it?"

That twin said, "Sylvester will."

I had thought that I was talking to Sylvester, but at that point I couldn't be sure, so when I spotted the other twin across the field, I headed right toward him, but got interrupted by Cookie giving me hello for the day. When I approached the twin who I thought was the one who had been across the field, I asked, "Did you get it yet?", and he answered "Sylvester will."

"But you're Sylvester!" I yelled. "I know that I've already asked each of you at least once to bring it."

He smiled and said, "I told you that Sylvester will."

"You wait right here," I said, and I set my hands on both sides of him and gave him a little shove downward to try and plant him there before I ran over to the other side of the field to get the other twin. I grabbed the other twin by the wrist and ran with him back toward where I had left the one who had just said, "Sylvester will." Only he was gone.

In a voice that was *fortissimo* with anger I said to the twin that I had just brought from the other side of the field, "Give it to me." And he said, "Sylvester will."

The other twin came back now and stood there smiling. Grinning like Flipper.

"All right, you guys," I screamed, "which one of you is Sylvester?"

Cookie came to my rescue. "I guess that today they've both decided to be Simon. Sometimes they do that." Then she walked up to them and commanded, "Smile!" They already were smiling, but they somehow made their smiles even bigger. Cookie pulled one of them by the belt and said, "This is the real Sylvester."

And both the twins began laughing so hard that they hugged and leaned on each other. You have to be real relaxed to laugh that hard. I wanted my magazine. "C'mon now; give it to me."

"We'll wait here while you get it from Julio's room," she directed. While they were gone, Cookie taught me how to never get them mixed up again.

Actually, there were only little differences between them. You couldn't tell who was running the bases. You had to be up close to tell them apart. And they had to smile, for Sylvester has five incisors on his bottom gum, and Simon has the normal four. If it helps you, remember that Simon has an *o* in it and so does *four*, which is the number of teeth. Sylvester has an *e* and so does *five* (for teeth). Simon and Sylvester didn't even have different personalities; they both enjoyed mischief, and they were both very good-natured. It was hard to stay angry at them even when the mischief was against you. Also, they enjoyed having each other. Being separated in school is the only being separated they ever adjusted to. A school principal started that in first grade.

Aunt Thelma talked a long time about how bad it was for them to be so inseparable and how they would never develop individual personalities, but I say that Aunt Thelma should be so lucky. Or me. It wasn't as if they absolutely adored each other; I'd seen them quarrel. It wasn't as if they were each one half making a whole; it was like one and one making two, and two is a good number to face the world with. As a matter of fact, I think that's the reason so many people get married, and as a matter of fact, I think that's the reason I wanted to get Hersch back.

Simon and Sylvester returned with my magazine. I thanked them before I asked for my quarter change. One of the twins said, "We'll match you double or nothing. Simon has your quarter. If you tell us which one is Simon, we'll pay you fifty cents. If you can't pick out Simon, we'll keep the quarter." They looked at each other and grinned. I guessed wrong, but that was the last time I ever did. I knew that they wouldn't have been able to ante up the extra quarter if I had guessed right.

Cookie walked me part way home. After she headed back toward the Projects, I examined my purchase. The girl in the center fold had reddish hair. After a while I noticed that she had fixed her hair in different styles for different poses. That was silly.

Getting *Playgirl* into the house was an easy caper, men. I placed the magazine in my mitt, after being careful to make it into a firm, tight roll. I draped my sweat jersey over the sticking-out end. Casually I called "hi" as I entered the house and bounded up the stairs to my room. Fortunately, that didn't take long since it is only a half-flight. I stowed the merchandise between the mattress and spring of my bed. Bottom left-hand corner.

In some silent way practices at the Projects had promoted me from a C— to a B+ and sometimes an A— player. I think that regular practices with the team had helped in an out-loud way, but they had probably helped the other kids more. To the world we were known as the B'nai B'rith team, but to us we were the B'nai Bagels.

My mother was something of a comical genius on the practice field. She could nag those kids in such a way that they thought that it was fun. One of

Mother's big manias was to have each kid lengthen his stride. "C'mon," she'd yell, "stretch those legs. Three steps take less time than four; two take less than three. C'mon, you guys, take a giant step." The Bagels would tease her and say, "May I?" And Mother would play it straight and answer, "Of course."

Another of her specialties was fielding. "Back up your man!" "Call your balls! Call your balls!" And then Sonefield would say, "Matzo balls!" and some-one else would yell "Ding dong balls!" but they would be catching like crazy as they did it.

If Mother was the comical captain, Spencer was the tough drill sergeant, and, strangely enough, the kids loved that, too. We practiced twice a week and after each session you could feel your muscles loosen and your nerves tighten. Our fielding became like some complicated dance number, the timing was so good. Spencer's having been catcher on his Little League Championship Team helped, too. He remem-bered how he felt *at first*; that kind of remembering is unusual in older brothers, especially when they are as old as Spencer. But he remembered how heavy the catcher's equipment felt, and how you wished that you could sight the ball from behind the plate as well as you can when it is coming toward you in the outfield. And he remembered what a nervous-maker it was to have that bat swinging in front of your eyes. Right in front. And how that made the ball even harder to sight. So what Spencer did was to train a catcher for us. He trained Hersch, who took it very well.

Spencer also made us practice bunting even though it quickly became obvious that Barry was the only kid who could pick a spot to lay down a bunt and beat it out. It should have happened to some nicer guy because Barry resented bunting the way I resent having to wear rubbers when I don't really believe it will rain and would like to take my chances with shoes. Barry always thought he could get a big hit.

Spencer's proclamation that everyone should walk to the playing field cut down on the number of parents who came. Mrs. Polsky came with Mrs. LaRosa, though. Sidney and Louis walked, and their mothers drove alongside in the Polsky's VW. They had to drive so slowly that the car never got out of first gear and their coming was announced by the erg-erg-erg sound getting louder and louder. Barry's mother also came to all the practices; she watched her son as if he were Macy's Thanksgiving Day Parade. The whole parade. Did you ever get the feeling about a guy that everything he does is rehearsed? Like the way Barry walked. I got the feeling that he had watched baseball movies and practiced that loose-jointed kind of saunter. Maybe a baseball uniform just makes you look that way. Maybe I even looked that way as I left the field. I wouldn't mind if I did.

Long before our first game came along, everyone on our team was in love with my mother. They called her Mother Bagel, and they called Spencer Brother Bagel. They preferred Mother to Brother, which wasn't exactly one of the Great Decisions of the Western World. But it does show that they had quite forgotten that she is a woman.

Simon and Sylvester, who are Catholic and who used to cross themselves before each time at bat, began tipping their hats to the Big Light Fixture in the sky. It wasn't that Mother did anything to convert them, it's just that kids have a way of imitating people they like. That's how Si and Syl probably began crossing themselves in the first place; they saw some ball player doing it on TV. Everyone including mother was having great trouble telling which was where on the field. They each had a number: Simon was Number 5, and Sylvester was Number 4, but Mother always had to check her list to see which number belonged to which. She finally brought a red handkerchief and made Simon wear it in his back pocket, but it was always falling out, and Mother couldn't remember whether she had assigned the handkerchief to Simon or to Sylvester. And sometimes for fun Sylvester would pick it up and wear it. Mother ended up addressing either or both of them as Twin. All she knew was that they were terrific.

Of all the kids who loved my mother, Sidney Polsky loved her best. Mother had been the first to call a spade a spade and fat, fat. Maybe Sidney didn't know that he was fat because no one had ever told him that before; his mother had banned the word from the entire language. I can see her now, changing all her recipes to "fry the potatoes in Crisco plump." After Sidney realized that what he was was fat, he began to lose weight, and Mother congratulated him after each pound he lost. The polite thing to do would have been to ignore his losing weight because you were supposed to have ignored that he was fat in the first place. But Sidney reported to Mother each pound he lost, and Mother reported to the team, and we all cheered. I mentioned how Mother's enthusiasm was a hard thing to be up against.

The kids loved it, and it made them love Sidney. He was looking better on the ball field, too. Partly because of Spencer's coaching, partly because of Mother's enthusiasm, and partly because of his mother's hiring a baseball tutor for him.

Aunt Thelma came to all but one of the pre-season practices. Even Spencer got used to having her around. She now wore golf shoes instead of high heels. Aunt Thelma did help out being that she liked to talk about her two specialties: raising children and educating them. Mother and Spencer would sometimes turn business over to Aunt Thelma if the parents wanted to talk deeply about their kids.

It turned out that nobody ever changed anybody's mind about anything. Grown-ups don't get talked into an idea. They get talked into adjusting to it. And that was Aunt Thelma's new greatest specialty. Mother was captain, Spencer was sergeant, and Aunt Thelma was chaplain.

9

WE WON OUR FIRST GAME. DAD'S STRATEGY PAID OFF;
Mom's nagging paid off; Spencer helped; and the Our
Lady of Mercy catcher helped, too. The Our Lady
of Mercy catcher couldn't. Our team stole home
three times. Once on a wild pitch, and the other two
times on normal mistakes. And in Little League mistakes are normal especially during the first game of
the season. The score was 7-2. We would have had
one more run if I hadn't watched to see where the
ball was going; it was two outs when Barry hit the
ball. I was on second at the time, and I should have
begun running immediately, but I waited to see
whether the ball would land on the ground or in a
glove. They were so slow fielding that I could have

made it home if I hadn't waited. It cost us a run, but it didn't cost us the game. And I guess I called my attention to it louder than Mother or Spencer did. As we left the field, Spencer said, "Let's run on those long flies with two outs. Got nothing to lose, kid." I wondered if Spencer knew how much more embarrassed I was than either Botts or Hersch or any non-relative would have been.

All the parents and spectators on our side came swooping down on the field as Mother was yelling, "Do you like the feeling?"

Everyone chorused, "Yeah!"

As the parents and spectators arrived, Mother and Spencer were shaking the boys' hands and patting them on their backs and telling them encouraging little things. Mother patted Sidney on his plump and said, "Five more pounds off that, and you're going to be the fastest thing on our team."

Mrs. Polsky took Sidney's hand and jerked him around and said to Mother, "You are more concerned about my Sidney's width than I am."

And Mother answered, "That's all right. I don't mind. Think nothing of it."

Mrs. Polsky poked a hole in the air with her chin and marched Sidney toward the exit.

The Our Lady of Mercy coach came over to Mother. "That was a good game, Mrs. Setzer."

"Terrific. Simply terrific," Mother admitted.

"That's quite a nice little pitcher you have there."

"Got another one just as good. Got two. Twins. They're terrific. Simply terrific."

"Your catching was good. Very good."

"Terrific. Simply terrific," Mother repeated.

Spencer didn't have Mother's ability to have one hundred per cent joy. He always sprinkles a mountain of joy with some worry like pepper over mashed potatoes. So he said to the Our Lady of Mercy coach, "We need to improve our batting some."

The coach said, "Yes, you will when you meet the Elks. You'll need some good batting for them."

"Aren't they the League Champs?" Mother asked.

"They're terrific. Simply terrific," the coach said.

"We'll be terrific -er," Mother answered. Mother wanted undiluted joy. Mother was not a gracious winner.

We worked like something beautiful on the field. Mother would meet with us before each game and tell what she planned to do; she met with us after the game to tell us what we had done wrong. She wasn't gentle; neither was Spencer. They were sure of themselves, and it got results. We won our second game and our third. And then we lost our fourth game to the Elks, and we felt rotten. Mother had wanted that, too. She and Spencer analyzed and scolded and made us work harder, and we won again.

She had made the team care, and she (and Spencer) had given us enough training to make it count.

A lot of the mothers cared, too. Too much. Too many phone calls worth. When your mother is manager and your brother is coach, the phone rings a lot. Often it is just to find out what time the game or practice is. Often it was Mrs. Polsky, wanting to know something like could she get an extra uniform for Sidney because she didn't think it was sanitary for him to have only one uniform the whole year. She had forgotten all the trouble we had getting his pants in the first place.

Very often it was Mrs. Jacobs. When I knew that it was Mrs. Jacobs calling, I listened in on the extension. She sure knew how to stick up for her kid. I would be embarrassed to have my mother take such good care of me.

MOTHER: Yes, Mrs. Jacobs. (That's when I picked up the extension phone. Quietly. It's an easy caper.)

MRS. JACOBS: Mr. Jacobs and I are somewhat concerned about Barry's attitude toward these practices, Bessie. Barry seems less eager to practice this year. He seems to feel that he is being held back.

MOTHER: Really, Mrs. Jacobs, I had no idea. You tell Barry that if he is being held back, *retained* they call it now, Mrs. Jacobs, he shouldn't come to practice at all. Not at all. School work comes first.

MRS. JACOBS: I was not referring to his school work, Bessie. My Barry is a straight-A student. I am referring to his work on the baseball field. You keep telling him to choke up on the bat, and you keep making him practice bunting. How can he make home runs that way? Last year he was the star homer hitter on the B'nai B'rith team, and I know he would like to be again this year.

MOTHER: Mrs. Jacobs, he can hit homers all he wants to in the games. That is, when he's given the signal to hit. Right now I want he should learn other things. That way, when he gets other signals, he can do other things. Like bunting is other things.

MRS. JACOBS: Do you think that bunting is the right thing to do? After all, you are holding him back.

MOTHER: Strategy it is, Mrs. Jacobs. Until the season is over, I won't know if it's the right thing to do.

MRS. JACOBS: It's so hard on him, a boy used to being champion. . . .

MOTHER: My pot is burning on the stove, Mrs. Jacobs, and my arm is not long enough to . . .

Spencer had come into the office and saw me carefully replacing the receiver of the extension phone. "For crying out loud, Mark, don't tell me that you listen in on phone calls."

"How else will I know if it's about me?"

"*About* you isn't the same thing as *for* you. What's the matter with you, kid, don't you think Mother and I have enough trouble with the overlaps?"

"What do you mean, overlaps?"

"I mean the parts of you that . . . oh! just skip it, kid. Just skip it." Spencer left the office fast and me confused.

10

EVEN AFTER THE SEASON OFFICIALLY BEGAN, I CON-
tinued going to the Projects on Saturdays. After
those first two times, I went in the afternoons. Every
Saturday, and usually on Sundays, too, even if I
wasn't buying *Playgirl.* I went until the incident with
Botts. There was something about handling a ball
there at the Projects that was like magic. The ball
would come to me: in my mitt if I was fielding or
square onto my bat if I was batting. At Little League
I was like a watched kettle; I got hot, but I never got
up enough steam to boil. I was better than average.
Better enough than average to be in the starting line-
up even though Mother and Spencer never worked
with me at home, the way I had thought they would.

99

And I no longer wanted them to. When I played at the Projects, I wasn't anybody's pupil or somebody's brother or someone's son. I was myself, and I liked that. I felt guilty for sometimes preferring the Projects to the Bagels.

The thing with Botts happened late in June, more than three-quarters of the way through our season. Cookie had made a habit of walking me part of the way home. Every time she would ask me to bring back my good jacket, the one whose lining I had ripped. Finally, one Saturday I remembered, and I brought it in a brown paper bag. And that was the last Saturday I went to the Projects.

Who would ever have taken Cookie's walking me part way home seriously? Certainly not me. Cookie was like a puppy or a mascot or something. After the first week I mostly forgot that she was a girl. Except when she smiled. One time I had asked the kid with the beginnings of a beard why it was that everyone listened to Cookie. (He really ought to have started shaving. He didn't look kempt.) He explained that there were seven Riveras; six of them were boys. Cookie had to do a lot around the house. She was a little bit spoiled, being the only girl, but only a little bit; being that she worked so hard around the house, I guess she deserved it.

On the Saturday it happened with Botts I had gotten into the game right away. Botts had been waiting and my arrival made an even number. Our teams were not full count, and the guys in the outfield had to cover a lot of ground. Which they did. I dropped one fly ball, but since it didn't break a window or anything, the only comment was *Stupid* and *Greasyfingers*. At first I tried to say something in my own defense, but they didn't care; they just wanted to pitch the next ball, and we all had to concentrate on that. It was great not having an audience.

Then Fortune came down and called time out.

Just like that.

And everyone took time out.

Just like that.

"I want to see Mark Bagel," she said.

I walked over to her. "There was already an even number when I got here."

"I'm not playing today, anyway," she answered. "I came down to fix your jacket. Did you bring it in that bag I saw you carrying in?"

"Oh, yeah. Almost forgot. Just a minute, you guys," I called as I ran to get the bag.

Simon, who was due up at bat, got impatient. "Really, Cookie," he said, "Why do we all have to take time out while you woo with Mark?"

He shouldn't have said that. Sylvester began singing, "Woo woo woo-ooo-ooo."

And that was all it took for the others to pipe in.

"Go along and play," I yelled. "I'll be up for my time at bats."

Cookie pulled a needle and thread out of her pocket. The right color. And I had worn it only those first times; she had remembered the color. The jacket had been a present from Aunt Thelma: navy blue with silver buttons and a scarlet lining. The best I had ever had.

Cookie sewed invisibly. You could hardly see where it had been ripped. "Where did you learn to sew?" I asked.

"Guess I was just born to it. Mother works in a girdle factory. She sews the elastic across the tops."

"Oh," I said. "Must be interesting work."

"I don't know why you'd think that. It's a job."

"Well, there are all those different sizes and all," I stammered.

"That's nothing. The big ones need big elastic and the small ones need small elastic. It's that simple." She handed me my jacket.

"Say, thanks. Thanks a lot. You sure have a talent for sewing."

"I am also excellent at drawing and arithmetic. I speak Spanish as excellent as I do English. I make marshmallow fudge, and I can hold my breath to a count of eighty-five—if you count fast."

She turned and started back upstairs.

"Cookie!" I yelled.

"Your time at bat, Setzer. C'mon, let's make it count."

"Just a minute, you guys." And I began to run after Cookie, yelling, "I brought you something."

The whole gang heard me. Which wasn't very hard because I didn't exactly whisper. You don't whisper when you're trying to get a guy's attention out in the open air. Or a girl's.

Cookie stopped and turned around and smiled. Her smile sort of dawns on her face; it starts as a small streak and then lights up everything. It's like announcing daybreak. Even if her mouth is too big.

I dug my hand into the bag and took out what I had brought. Cookie held out her hand, and something about the way she did it made me slip it onto her forefinger.

"A bagel," I explained. "It's to eat."

She looked up at me and still looking at me began to nibble around the edge as she held it on her forefinger.

"It's delicious," she said.

"It's delicious-er with cream cheese," I said.

I should have noticed how quiet the whole gang had been. That would have given me a good idea that they were watching us. But I guess I was so interested in Cookie's reaction to the bagel and that smile and all that I didn't pay any real attention. Until they began that chanting again. "Woo woo wooo-ooo-ooo." They kept it up.

"Cut it out, you guys," I said.

They kept it up.

Botts broke out of the rhythm by calling out, "Is that why you never buy a look at my magazine? Be-

cause you've got a girl of your own?"

"Don't be silly," I said. "I don't have a girl. I have my own copy."

"I'll just bet," he smirked.

"I do, too. I'll bring it. I'll show you."

"I'm going to tell you something, Setzer. And I'm going to tell you good. You better never bring that magazine around here. You hear me?"

"I hear you," I said. "I imagine that the kids up on Crescent Hill can hear you. Now, you hear me. Quit calling Cookie my girl. She just did me a favor."

"Yeah, a favor," he said. "Is that why you slipped a bagel over her finger? . . . *and with this bagel I do thee wed . . .*"

"Cut that out," I yelled. By this time Botts and I were kind of separated from the rest of the gang. Cookie walked up to Botts and stretched her neck so that she was practically nose to nose with him. She said, "Botts, you drop this subject. Drop it right now. Because if you don't, I'm going to tell your mother and your aunt what you do with your money. And what you do with your time. I know, and I'll tell."

"You wouldn't dare."

"I would."

"They won't believe you."

"They will," she said softly and calmly. We knew, as Botts must have known, that she would dare tell, and that they would believe.

Botts blinked his eyes fast; his shoulders and chin

dropped. The whole gang saw it, Botts backing down. Cookie shouldn't have done that even if she did it for me, and even if she did it to a louse like Franklin P. Botts.

He turned on me. "You just better never bring that magazine around here, Setzer. You cut in on my territory, and I'll liquidate you."

When a guy isn't on TV and he uses a word like *liquidate* to another guy, he comes off pretty silly.

I laughed.

Botts socked me.

I'm not great at hand-to-hand combat, so I was slow winding up. Simon pulled on Botts, and I felt Sylvester pinning my arms back.

"Break it up. Break it up," they yelled together.

Botts, with his arms pinned back and his neck stretched out, yelled again, "Wattcha gonna do, Setzer? Tell your mother and have me kicked off the team?"

"That's what you deserve," I said. "But I'm no squealer. I won't tell." The B'nai Bagels certainly deserved better than him, I thought. If my mother had not been manager, I probably would have told on him, but I couldn't. He knew that.

"Go ahead and tell," he teased. "See if I care."

"I'm not going to tell. You just quit poking fun at other people like Cookie."

"Why ya so worried about Cookie? Cookie *is* your girl. Woo woo wooo . . ."

I freed one arm and landed it in Botts' stomach. It didn't have much punch, though, so much of the muscle having been wasted in freeing it from Sylvester.

Simon spoke up. "Now you're even. Let's finish the game. You're at bat, Setzer." He let Botts go after saying that.

And Sylvester added, "Hey, Cookie, how about your not calling times-out any more?"

Cookie sniffed the air. "O.K., I won't call times-out when it's times-out for supper, either."

"You know what Syl means," Simon scolded.

"O.K.," Cookie said. She looked at me and said, "Thanks for the bagel, Mark." She looked at Botts and said something in Spanish. I would write what she said, but I don't know Spanish, and I've already included enough foreign words like *haftorah*.

Botts didn't understand Spanish either. Cookie looked up at Botts and smiled and said, "O.K.?" That smile!

Botts softened. "O.K.", he answered.

Cookie walked toward their building.

"What did she say?" Botts asked. No one answered. "What did that mean?"

"Skip it," Sylvester said.

"C'mon now, you guys, what does that mean?"

The big kid said, "Cookie told you that . . ."

Simon interrupted, "Let's play ball."

"I wanna hear," Botts urged. "What did she say?"

The kid with the beard continued, "She said, 'If brains were Holy Water, you wouldn't have enough to baptize a mosquito.' "

Simon and Sylvester poked the ground with their toes. The big kid laughed, and so did I. That Cookie was a clever guy.

Botts looked from the big kid to me and then squinted his eyes and said, "Watch it, Jew Boy. Watch who you're laughing at."

And that's the way it happened. That's the way it is with kids like Botts. The feeling is always there. Like bacteria, just waiting for conditions to get dark enough to grow into a disease.

I picked up my jacket and went home.

11

I ASKED HERSCH OVER THE NEXT SATURDAY. IT HAD been a long time since we had spent an afternoon together. Baseball and Bar Mitzvahs and practicing at the Projects had used up a lot of my time and Hersch's Crescent Hill friend had used up a lot of his.

We walked to my house after services. There were long pauses along the way. In the talking, not the walking. I half-hoped he'd bring up the subject of Barry, but I other half-hoped he wouldn't. When you don't like a guy, and you tell another guy about it, it's hard to be natural with either one afterwards. I wondered if that were true for Hersch; I wondered if he felt peculiar when I was with him and Barry because I knew all the things he used to say about

Barry during the sarcastic game. The funny thing is that you can not like someone and still be curious about him. Be especially curious about him. Barry was like that awful gasoline commercial on television. I hated that commercial worse than anything, yet I would walk from the bedroom to the living room to see it. To see if it was really that bad. I couldn't understand that about myself.

Well, the conversation didn't get around to Barry. As I said, it hardly got around. Friendship should be daily. Like how my mother and father didn't run out of things to say to each other. And how my mother could talk on the telephone for twenty-five minutes at a time with Aunt Thelma who she talks to almost every day, but she never got beyond, "Fine how are you? Fine. The boys are fine. Yes, we're all fine," when she called long distance to her brother in Wisconsin. You'd think they'd have a lot to say to each other, having stored things up between calls.

Now Hersch and I were on long distance, and it didn't used to be that way.

After we got to my house I asked him if he would like a game of Monopoly.

"Oh, all right," he answered.

I wondered why he said the *oh*. I was probably boring him, but I got the game out of the closet anyway, being that I couldn't come up with a better idea. We began playing, but it turned out to be the worst kind of game: slow and silent.

Mother came upstairs to my room and interrupted with, "Well, Herschie, how nice that you should come play with my Moshe." Now, she could have gone all the rest of her life without saying that. Why should a guy's mother thank someone for playing with the guy?

Hersch answered his shoes, "I've been busy."

"Your baseball, Herschie, has improved one hundred eighty-five per cent. Quite a little catcher, you've become. I just may put you in as a tournament player."

Hersch smiled. "That would be great. What about Barry? Will Barry make it, too?"

"About Barry, I'm not too sure. The twins are better."

"But, Mrs. Setzer, they're only eleven years old. They can have a chance next year. This would be Barry's last chance; he feels that he would be champion hitter on another team."

"That may be true," Mother said, "because for batting, Botts beats Barry. Maybe on some other team, he wouldn't have such a competition, and he would be best. But I say that if the tournament needs batting, I'll give them the best we have, and that would be Botts. Barry for bunting; Botts for batting."

Hersch said, "If you didn't make Barry a bunting specialist, he would beat Botts at batting."

Mother looked hurt. "Who told you that?"

Hersch answered, "No one told me; Mrs. Jacobs

told my mother."

Mother quietly shook her head back and forth and said, "Oh, my. We'll see. We'll see."

It occurred to me that I could have put a quick end to Botts' chances as a tournament player, and it's probably true that one of the reasons that I kept quiet was because closing the door on Botts would have opened it for Barry. But I didn't create even a hint about Botts. And it wasn't easy. The words sat in my throat like a huge marshmallow, but I said nothing except ask Hersch if he wanted to finish Monopoly.

"Oh, I don't care. What else is there?"

That *oh* again. I was sure that I was boring him. Then I remembered. "Just a minute," I said.

I got up from the floor and closed my bedroom door very quietly. I smiled at Hersch as I stepped over the Monopoly board as well as his legs, and I lifted the skirt of my bedspread. From between the mattress and the box spring I pulled out my copy of *Playgirl*.

"How about that?" I couldn't keep from smiling.

Hersch looked over at me and back and said, "I've seen it."

"You've seen it?"

"Yeah, I've seen it," he repeated.

"Where did you see it?" I challenged.

"At Barry's."

"Barry Jacobs?"

"Yeah, Barry Jacobs. Which other Barry is there?"

"Where does he keep his?"

"On his desk."

"On his desk?" I asked. "You must mean *in* his desk."

"No. I said on his desk. That's where he keeps it. *On* his desk."

"In his bedroom?"

"That's where his desk is. You've been to his house. You know that's where his desk is."

I couldn't believe it yet. "Right on his desk? Right in his bedroom? He might as well keep it on the coffee table in the living room."

"Why should he? The family can buy its own copy."

"Well, keeping it out, practically in public like that! Doesn't his mother clean or anything? How come she didn't notice?"

"Who said she didn't notice? Of course she noticed. She bought him the subscription."

"Subscription?" I yelled. "You mean he gets *Playgirl* of the month every month?"

"Sure. The mailman brings it right to the house. Same as he does *Life* or *The Saturday Evening Post*."

"How come his mother bought him a subscription?"

"He wanted one for his birthday."

"Which birthday? His forty-second going on Bar Mitzvah?"

"Mrs. Jacobs doesn't want Barry to hide things

from her. She wants to know what he is doing all the time."

"She's nosey," I suggested.

"That's not it at all. Mrs. Jacobs is very intelligent. She used to be . . ."

"Be a schoolteacher," I finished.

"What's wrong with that? I think she's right. About hiding things."

"I don't know what's wrong with it. It just seems wrong. I don't want my mother looking at my *Playgirl.*"

"Why not?"

"Because it's mine, that's why."

And I put *my* magazine back between *my* mattress and *my* box spring of *my* bed. Never before was I that glad to have a corner that was all mine. Barry could have a subscription for twenty consecutive years. For fifty consecutive years until he needed bifocals to see the center fold, and I would rather have my one copy that is mine and that I didn't have to share with anyone unless I invited them.

I asked Hersch if he would like some lunch.

We ate peanut butter and jelly sandwiches on toast. When you have braces, it's easier to eat peanut butter sandwiches if the bread is toasted. As we ate, Hersch told me some things about his school. There was nothing the country mouse could tell that the Crescent Hill mouse didn't already know. I didn't feel too bad when his mother came for him.

Mrs. Miller said, "We'll have to arrange for Mark to spend an evening at our house." Mother answered, "That will be lovely." Mrs. Miller always said we'll have to arrange for Mark to spend an evening at our house, and Mother always said that will be lovely, and it never happened.

You can't cart friendship from place to place and lend it out like Hertz. Hersch rent-a-friend.

12

SPENCER CAME DOWN WITH THE FLU. MOTHER WAS
convinced he did it on purpose because he had mid-
term exams at summer school and he had been com-
plaining about not having enough time to study.
When the flu bug hit, we were one game out of first
place with two games to go to finish the season. We
had to beat the Elks; they had lost three games all
season. We had lost four; three of the games we lost,
we had lost to them. We would meet them again the
last game. To become league champions, then, we
had to win our next two games. The Elks were almost certain to win their next. Their opponent was
as bad as the B'nai B'rith had been the year before.
Our next game would be a tough one. Against the

Chicken Delights team. We had lost to them once already.

Mother scolded the kitchen light fixture, "Fever, you had to invent!" She was baking cookies for my Bar Mitzvah party. Baking and freezing. The kitchen was steaming with the odor of chocolate and jelly and nuts. I think my mother bakes because it occupies her hands and not her head; other mothers knit.

Mother yelled as I came in the door, "Don't touch. It's for the Bar Mitzvah!"

"Whose Bar Mitzvah?" I asked.

"You whose. That's whose," she answered.

"What I want to know is this: if it's my Bar Mitzvah, why can't I enjoy it now?"

"Because it's for the company. You want I shouldn't have enough and be embarrassed in front of the whole congregation?"

"Enough? You'd have enough if you stopped baking right now, and I ate half of what you already have."

"Don't underestimate your mother, Moshe. My cookies are so superb that everyone will help themselves. Three times and four times they'll take."

"So make them less good and share them with me now."

"You want me to offer up something less than the best? You talk like Cain. Now, go. Change your clothes. Mother is thinking."

I came back downstairs after I had changed my

clothes. Mother offered me a plate of edges and broken pieces. I looked down at them, up at her, and said, "You sure don't hesitate offering me second best."

"God, you're not," she answered. "Now eat. Quietly. Mother is worrying."

"What are you worrying about?"

"Your brother's forehead. He's got fever."

"He'll get over it," I said as I munched. Even the edges and crumbs were good. "He's strong headed."

"It's not fair about viruses living inside men. Do men live inside animals? Tell me." Mother was ceiling gazing again.

"How about Jonah living in that big fish for three days and three nights?" It was me answering, not the Deity.

"You call that living?" Mother asked.

"You asked, I answered."

"All right then, answer me this one. Who is going to help me manage our next game? Our next game is very important, I might add."

"I know, Mom. I know. Remember me? I'm on the team, too."

"Your brother has been very helpful to me. He knows the opponents better than I do. A memory he's got. Like an elephant."

"I'll bet Dad will give you a hand."

"He doesn't know the players. Besides, he's busy."

"What about Barry's mother? Or Sidney's? They come to all the games anyway."

Mother stopped scrubbing the cookie sheets, turned around, looked hard at me and didn't answer.

"Well, what about them?" I asked again.

"Don't talk with your mouth full."

I swallowed. "Why don't you ask them? Mrs. Jacobs or Mrs. Polsky?"

"Oh, I don't know," Mother answered.

"Why not?" I insisted.

Mother turned toward me very quickly, and in that very brief minute I caught a look of worry on her face. Worry and puzzle. It was the same look she used to have when she was discussing Spencer with Dad before we all got involved with baseball. And it was also the same look that she had when she finished a telephone call with Mrs. Polsky or Mrs. Jacobs. "Because," Mother said, turning back toward the sink and scrubbing at the cookie sheets again, "because I'm not sure they're on my side."

Aunt Thelma chose just that minute to walk in. Mother wiped her hands on a paper towel, gave the top of the stove a good rub with it before throwing it in the garbage, looked up at the kitchen ceiling, and said, "So, Casey Stengel she isn't, but she'll do." She sent a kiss to the Deity by closing her eyes and smacking her lips to the air between the light fixture and her upraised face.

"I was just on my way to the shopping center, and I thought I'd stop in to see if you needed anything. I don't know what made me come so far out of my way."

Mother looked at me and smiled. "We know, don't we, Moshe?" With that Mother grabbed her sister around the shoulder and said, "Thelma, about this game that's coming up."

The game was Tuesday evening. Aunt Thelma had come for supper. Mother carried a tray up to Spencer. He asked to see Aunt Thelma, too. The two of them sat at the foot of his bed and listened to him as if he were spreading wisdom instead of germs.

"Remember," he said, "start Burser pitching. If it's necessary to pull him out, use Simon. We have to keep Sylvester eligible for Friday's game. If he pitches today, he won't be eligible for four days. That would be Saturday. And our game against the Elks is Friday, and we need Sylvester then. Really need him then. The Elks' powerhouse, Stevens, Kunzciski, and Holden are all left handers. We need our left hander against them. Use Simon if you get in a pinch, but save Sylvester." He closed his eyes and collapsed against his pillow. "Save Sylvester," he repeated.

Mother and Aunt Thelma tiptoed out of the room as if they had just been given a message by Moses, via satellite from Mount Sinai. Spencer played his part. He kept his eyes closed as he lay against the pillow. I half expected a great billow of smoke and a voice from an echo chamber saying, "I have spoken." Only the fact that he was holding his fork in one fist and his knife in the other spoiled the picture.

For once you could tell that Aunt Thelma was Mother's sister. She was bouncing with enthusiasm—except Aunt Thelma was so skinny that she sprung more than she bounced. And the whole thing boiled down to them both bossing me around. Get the balls. Get the bats. Get the towels. Get moving.

By the time we got to the ball park I was ready to cheer for the other team, except that this year I never could be anything but a Bagel.

Cookie arrived to give Mother a message. "Simon can't come today."

"Why not?" Mother asked.

"Because he can't leave the house."

"Why not?"

"Because he keeps throwing up."

Mother looked up at the sky. "One virus is not enough? A D-Day invasion we had to have?"

Cookie looked unhappy. "Yep, the virus." Some people like to deliver bad news. Cookie didn't.

Mother didn't reply; she was either giving You-Know-Who a bawling out, or else she was calculating her strategy.

Cookie explained, "I did my best to get him well, Mother Bagel. But he just keeps throwing up, throwing up, throwing up. And you can't have him doing that in public. Throwing up, I mean."

"Wouldn't look nice at all," Mother said. She

smiled at Cookie.

"All we can hope for now," Cookie said, "is that the Elks catch it, too."

"That's not a very nice thing to wish," Mother scolded.

"All right, then. I wish Simon gets well and that Sylvester never catches it."

"That's better," Mother said.

Cookie paused a minute and said, "I think I was right the first time; it will be better if the Elks catch it." And she walked away from Mother.

I waved to Cookie by flapping my hand alongside my leg. She looked puzzled and copied the motion. Botts saw us; some guys can't keep their eyes to themselves.

Hal Burser's pitching was not the greatest; his arm usually gave out about the fifth inning, which is generally not too bad, because I noticed that the umpires usually gave out about the same time. Because that's when they began calling any close one a strike. This umpire was impressed with the importance of the game, and he called them all sincerely. The score was 5-3 in our favor in the fifth inning. Burser had just given up two hits after the Chicken Delights had two outs. His next pitch was wild. Hersch scurried around like a gray mouse in a grain field to get it, but both their runners made it home before it could be retrieved. They tied the score, and Aunt Thelma, who long ago in the season had forgotten all about one of the purposes of Little League being to teach boys to lose gracefully, called a hurried conference with Mother and Hal on the mound. I could tell that Aunt Thelma was ready to pull him out of the game. I could just tell. Mother put her arm around Hal's shoulder and talked to him quietly, and Hal nodded "yes" a few times. They left the mound, and Hal finished the inning with a strike out and the game tied up at 5-5.

It was the top of the sixth. One, two, three; Botts struck out. Sonefield hit a pop fly, and Mother realized that she would need some great pitching to save the game. She wanted Sylvester to warm up with Botts catching. She called for Botts, but he had disappeared. Aunt Thelma had seen him heading for the locker room, and she started straight for him. I guess she figured she should since she was hired to do Spencer's job, and Spence always retrieved little boys from the little boys' room. So she charged in like Papa Bear. She waddled out like Mother Goose, towing Botts with one hand and carrying a rolled-up copy of a magazine with the other. Her face was a special kind of red called furious, and Botts' was a special kind of pink called embarrassed. Guys who are brassy with kids their own age often are embarrassable with adults. Insincere guys, that is.

Not far behind Aunt Thelma came Sidney Polsky, looking down at the ground and shuffling his feet.

Sidney's mother began running along the bleacher parallel to the path to our dugout. "What's the matter, Sidney? What happened, Sidney? Sidney? Sidney, what happened in there? What's the matter, son?"

"Nothing's the matter, Mom. I'm fine," Sidney answered. Finally.

"What's in your hand, Sidney? Give it to Mother."

Sidney held up what was in his hand and gave it to his mother. It was a nickel.

"What's the matter, Sidney? Wasn't it enough? Do they cost a dime?"

"It's all right, Mom. Here. Take the nickel. It's all right."

"Sidney, here. Take another nickel. Mother will give another nickel. Go back in there, Sidney."

"I'm all right, Mom. Honest. I don't have to go back."

"Sidney, Mother says take the nickel."

"I don't need another nickel, Mom. It's free in there."

"Then why did you ask for a nickel in the first place?"

"I'll tell you later."

"Sidney, what was going on in there?"

"I'll tell you later."

Sidney escaped by disappearing into our dugout. Mrs. Polsky stood in the bleachers leaning down over the railing like an inverted *V*.

"Sidney, what is the meaning of all this?"

Cookie walked over and tapped Mrs. Polsky's inverted back. "He'll tell you later," she said.

Since we hadn't scored with our big power up at bat in the top of the sixth, Mother had to put Sylvester in to pitch in the bottom half of that inning, even without much warming up. If he could hold their team to five runs, and if we could score in the seventh, the game would be ours and Sylvester would have pitched only two innings, which would still leave him eligible for Friday. Four innings of pitching would make him ineligible until Saturday.

He gave up only one hit in the bottom of the sixth and thanks to our superb defense, the Chicken Delights didn't score. Unfortunately, neither did we in the next inning. The game was tied at 5-5, and we were in for extra innings.

What's a mother to do?

Take Sylvester out? There was no one to use in his place. The game was important; a win was necessary, and therefore, so was Sylvester. No runs in the eighth. Nothing in the ninth. We had a couple of hits, but nothing we could score on. Then Barry slammed a home-run in the tenth; he ran around touching all the bases, and he was mobbed as he headed for the dugout. Mother patted him on the back, and all the guys jabbed him on the shoulder or shook his hand or patted him. Even me. Even if it was Barry, it was my Bagels. And Aunt Thelma sure didn't look dignified springing up and down like that and waving *Playgirl* with the center fold picture coming unfurled and flapping in the breeze. As soon as she noticed what had happened, she rolled the whole thing up and stashed it under her arm and clapped her hands instead.

As we took the field for the bottom half of the inning that we hoped would finish the game, Barry said to Hersch, "I could have been doing that all season long if I hadn't been held back."

"Aw, Barry, you weren't held back."

"I was, too. Old Lady Bagel making me bunt and stuff." He knew he was talking loud enough for me to hear.

"It was her strategy, Barry. Look how it paid off."

"It would have paid off a lot sooner if she had let me try for homers more often."

"Last year you tried for homers all the time and look where we stood."

"Last year we didn't have the twins or Botts. Old Lady Bagel didn't make all that much difference."

"You can't say that. What's fair is fair." You could tell that Hersch was uncomfortable having Barry talk like that. He kept glancing over at me to see if I was listening.

Barry said, "What's fair may be fair. But what's a homer is a homer."

Even if what he said had been right, it couldn't

seem right as long as he called her Old Lady Bagel. It wasn't even witty.

Sylvester Rivera pitched his big heart out, and Barry's homer became the run that won us the game.

When we got home, Spencer was waiting in the living room in his bathrobe and bare feet. He looked like a cartoon drawing: gray and lumpy.

Aunt Thelma burst into the house waving the rolled-up *Playgirl*. "We won!" she yelled.

"We won. Spencer, put on your slippers," Mother said.

"What was the score?" he asked.

"Six to five, our favor; Mark, go get your brother's slippers."

"Who pitched?"

"Started Burser, but had to finish with Sylvester. Spencer, put a scarf around your throat."

"Sylvester? Did he go four innings?"

Mother nodded yes. Then said, "Spencer, don't walk around with the bathrobe open."

Spencer howled, "I told you to save Sylvester. My parting words to you were to save Sylvester. Thelma is my witness. What did I say, Thelma? Did I say to save Sylvester? Mark! Did you hear me? Didn't I say to save Sylvester?"

"I'll tell you all about it," Mother reasoned. "But you must not get overheated. Sit down, Spencer darling. Put on some socks, also."

Aunt Thelma looked at Spencer and said, "Very briefly, I'll tell you. What your mother did was necessary. Absolutely necessary. But I have something that I must discuss with your mother first. In private." She moved her eyes in my direction, then back to Mother and tilted her head.

I pretended I didn't notice. When one relative says "in private" to another relative in front of a child relative, it means that they want the child-type relative to leave the room. I didn't budge.

"Mark, go get a bath," Mother requested.

"What about Spencer?"

"He'll take his bath later," Mother answered.

"I mean how come Aunt Thelma isn't sending him out of the room? Why can't I listen?"

"Because it's not your business. Go, Mark. Be a good boy. Go take a bath."

"If it's about the team, it's my business."

"Your Aunt Thelma said 'in private.' Now, be a good boy. Go."

"I'm going. But under protest."

"For you to go is unusual. Under protest is nothing new."

Instead of taking a bath, I listened. If I had taken a bath every time Mother had sent me, I'd have been all puckered.

AUNT THELMA: What do you think that Botts boy was doing in the locker room?

MOTHER: Thelma, don't embarrass me. Don't ask.

AUNT THELMA: Guess.

MOTHER: What he does in the locker room is his business.

AUNT THELMA: Do you know? Do you have any idea of what his business is?

MOTHER: Locker room business. C'mon, Thelma, I asked that you shouldn't embarrass me.

AUNT THELMA: Well, he embarrassed me. His business is selling looks at *Playgirl*. For five cents a look. Sidney Polsky was his customer.

MOTHER: *Playgirl?* The magazine?

AUNT THELMA: Yes, that magazine with all the undressed girls.

MOTHER: Let me see it. (I heard the pages being flipped.) You know, I saw this magazine in my Moshe's room. Between the mattress and the spring. I thought that it must have something special in it and that was why he was hiding it.

AUNT THELMA: You mean you didn't look?

MOTHER: No, I didn't look. I figured there was something in it he didn't want me to see. That's why he hid it. Spencer, did you know about this magazine?

SPENCER: Let me see it. (Long pause. Pages being flipped, being flipped, being flipped.) Ah. Ah. I'm familiar with the publication.

AUNT THELMA: Then why did you have to look at it if you're already familiar with it?

MOTHER: Because he likes it, that's why. Now, getting back to Botts and Polsky. So what? One was buying, and one was selling.

AUNT THELMA: Bess, you astound me. You know that your son is hiding something from you, and you don't do anything about it.

MOTHER: Thelma, every boy needs to have a little something to hide from his mother. I know I raised him right so far; he's not hiding LSD, and he's not smoking cigarettes and flushing them down the toilet. I figure if he wants a corner of privacy between the mattress and springs of his bed, that's fine with me. If it were something dangerous or illegal, I'd interfere, but a magazine? He deserves.

AUNT THELMA: Aren't you worried that if he gets away with that, he'll try something worse next year?

MOTHER: I'm more worried that if he finds that he can't have that little corner of privacy at home, he'll look somewhere else for it. Bumming around with bad kids or staying out all night, or trying to do something really secret and really bad. If it becomes something worse, I'll step in.

AUNT THELMA: Why don't you just buy him the magazine?

MOTHER: Because it's not my place to give him permission to be a peeping tom into *Playgirl*. Just because I let him doesn't mean that I have to approve, does it? I don't have to approve of everything he does, do I? And I have to save my hard disapproving for the bad things.

AUNT THELMA: You would never have allowed Spencer to get away with such nonsense.

MOTHER: Such nonsense he didn't want. With him it was French postcards he bought in some novelty store on Broadway in New York. And it was under the drawer lining instead of under the mattress.

SPENCER: You mean you knew I had those?

MOTHER: Of course. If you were a little bit more tidy, Mother wouldn't have had to straighten your drawers. I came running with them to your father, and he taught me. He said that you were trying privacy on for size, and if I didn't let you have a little when you were little, and a little more later, I would be encouraging you to become a sneak. And Dad predicted that you would become very good at it, being a sneak. He convinced me, your father. So I wiped all my fingerprints off the bellies of those ladies and put them back under the drawer lining. (I heard the pages being flipped again.) I must say, though, that Mark seems to have better taste. These girls are better looking than the ones you had on the postcards.

SPENCER: They didn't publish that magazine nine years ago. There's nothing wrong with my taste in women.

MOTHER: Offended, he is.

AUNT THELMA: Oh, yes. Offended. That's what I wanted to talk to you about. I know someone who is going to be very offended about what happened in the locker room today.

MOTHER: Who?

(*The phone rang just then and Mother answered. Oh, hello, Mrs. Polsky.*)

AUNT THELMA: That's who.

And I heard the door close as she left. I ran the water for my bath and didn't hear anything more than the water and the sounds in my head reviewing the conversation that had just finished downstairs and comparing it with what Hersch had told me about Barry's subscription. My mother may not have pronounced what she said as nicely as Mrs. Jacobs would have, but Mrs. Jacobs would never have said anything that nice. Sometimes I thought that Mrs. Jacobs should be more like my mother.

13

BETWEEN THE GAMES ON TUESDAY AND FRIDAY SAT Wednesday's Hebrew lesson. Everyone was congratulating Barry on his great hit, which won the game for us. You would never have known that Hersch and I had also played in the game.

"Well, Hersch," I said as we walked down the corridor to class, "what did you do last Tuesday after supper?"

"I was catcher in a terrific game of baseball," he said. "Let me tell you about it. The game went ten innings, and I caught from first inning to last. What did you do?"

Hersch's tone told me; I fell into my German accent. "Nossing much. I alzo played in a game of baseball. My game vent ten inninks alzo. I got vun sinkle and drove in vun run. Vhere vas your game?"

"It was at the Holy Child Playing Field. Where was yours, pray tell?"

"Alzo at the Holy Chilt Playink Field. Funny, I got ze funny feelink zat ze only person zere vas Barry Jacobs."

"That's strange. I had the same feeling. Do you suppose we could ever play with him?"

"Velll . . ." I said as I stroked my chin.

"Naw," he answered. "We're not in his league. We just happen to be on the same team."

And then we yukked until the rabbi said, "Gentlemen, if I may interrupt your discussion of Little League with a lesson about a few big leaguers like Moses and a different Aaron." It was the rabbi who had a supreme gift for sarcasm. Like him calling us *gentlemen*.

Hersch actually waited for me when class was over, and we began walking down the hall together.

"Did your mother pick the tournament players yet?"

"She vill zend to zem only Barry. Zat is as gut as hafink ze whole team from ze B'nai Bagels."

Hersch said, "Seriously, Mark, has she picked her players?"

Hersch was done playing the sarcastic game, but I didn't have sense enough to realize it. I felt terrible. Here I was on the verge of winning him back, and I was about to bollix up the whole thing, so I answered him straight. "I don't know."

"C'mon now, if she picked them, you'd know." He must have thought that I was still kidding around.

"Honest, Hersch, I don't know."

"I'll bet you don't. You just won't tell."

"I'm telling the truth, Hersch. I don't even know if she picked them or if she didn't pick them. Let alone know who is and who is not."

"You trying to tell me that she didn't talk it all over with you?"

"Any time my mother wants to discuss baseball, it's with my brother, and she sends me out of the room. I've been sent out of the room so often lately that I've worn a hole in the carpet."

"My parents used to send me out of the room a lot, too, but I'm breaking them of the habit. I think the best way to be is like Barry's folks. Barry's parents tell him everything, discuss everything in front of him, and he tells them everything, too. Sometimes he tells me things they say, too. Like he told me that Mrs. Polsky called after last night's game. She was real upset about Botts' selling Sidney a look at *Playgirl*."

"Yeah, I guess she's easily upset."

"Barry said that Mrs. Polsky had to worm the information out of Sidney. Barry's mother never has to worm information out of him. He can tell his mother everything without being afraid. I'll bet you don't tell your mother everything just because you're afraid to."

"Of course I'm afraid to tell her some things. And some other things are just my own business. Like what happened to me with Botts. I have to keep separate what happens to me as a kid and what happens to me as the guy whose mother manages the team."

Hersch buzzed in on Botts. "What happened to you with Botts? Mrs. Polsky sure would be interested in finding out. She wants to get some goods on Botts."

I shrugged my shoulders. "Skip it."

"C'mon, Moshe. You can tell me. What did that Botts do? Was it about the magazine? Mrs. Polsky told Mrs. Jacobs that if she ever found that magazine around the Little League field again, she'd confiscate it as evidence."

"Evidence for what?"

"I sure don't know. Barry didn't tell me that. He said that his mother talked to Mrs. Polsky a long time."

Hersch paused a minute and added, "That Botts sure is an operator. What did he ever do to you? Was it about the magazine?"

"Only indirectly."

"C'mon, Moshe. Tell me. Please?"

And like a dope, I told him. I just fell back into feeling buddies with Hersch again. It was the kind of talking we were doing. We used to do a lot of talking like that. That's one of my big weaknesses: instant trust. That's me: dehydrated friendship. Just add the proper amount of soothing waters, and I swell into the jolly green giant. Ho. Ho. Ho.

Hersch said immediately, "You better tell your mother. Prejudiced guys like that shouldn't be allowed on the team."

"I don't want to tell my mother."

"You're just chicken. You're afraid."

"I am not afraid to tell. I just don't want to. After all, you can't kick a guy off the team for something he did in his own yard. I was telling you that it's hard to keep separate what happens to me as a guy and what happens to me as a guy whose mother manages his team. It's the overlaps that are hard."

"Overlaps? What do you mean?"

"Overlaps," I repeated. And then I heard the echo. *Overlaps.* I knew now what Spencer meant. Only his problem was keeping brother and coach separate, and mine was keeping son and player and brother and player separate. Come to think of it, I had twice what he did.

"I'll tell you what I'll do," Hersch offered. "I'll tell Barry; he's sure to tell his mother. His mother is sure to tell your mother. See? That way your mother finds out, and you haven't squealed at all."

"You better not tell anyone. I mean *anyone,* Hersch."

"I sure am going to watch that Botts carefully from now on. One false move, or the first anti-Semitic word from him, and he's out. I'm going to tell

Barry to watch out, too. I won't tell him what happened. I'll just tell him to watch Botts."

I saw red. I saw purple. I got so mad, I saw red and purple tiger zigzags. "Don't let Barry know anything. Don't you dare! Don't you even hint!"

"What are you so excited about? Why are you covering up for a louse like Botts?"

"I am not covering up. Gosh, Hersch, don't you understand anything anymore? I told you about my awkward position. My telling would be worse than someone else's telling. It wouldn't be right."

"And I guess it's right for a guy like that to be on the team and get all its benefits."

"It's more like fair and unfair than right and wrong. I said that I wouldn't tell my mother, and I won't. Botts likes my mother. I'll bet half the time he forgets she's Jewish. Half the time is a start for him, don't you think?"

"You sure you're not telling just because you're afraid?"

"Of course I'm not sure. I just can't handle the overlaps. Promise that you won't tell, Hersch. Not Barry. Not his mother. Not your mother. Not anyone."

Hersch raised his hand and said, "I do solemnly swear not to tell the truth, the whole truth, and nothing but the truth about Franklin P. Botts." He smiled, and it was the smile that he used to answer the door with at his old house. I knew he wouldn't tell.

14

SO IT HAPPENED THAT GOING INTO THE LAST GAME OF
our season, we were tied with the Elks. By a miracle
they had lost their last game. It wasn't exactly a miracle; it was the virus. Two of their three great left
handers had gotten it. Our last game would determine
the league championship. It seems to me the reason
last games that break a tie for championship happen
so often in stories is that they happen so often in real
life.

By Friday the virus had left town. Everyone was
better. Including Spencer. Including Simon. And including the two star left handers from the Elks.
Mother was so nervous that she burnt the goulash.

"What happened?" Spencer asked; he shouldn't

have.

"Listen, Mr. Betty Crocker," Mother said, "from Ford Frick you wouldn't expect a perfect goulash."

"All I did was to ask what happened."

"It's a confederacy," Mother said.

"You mean *conspiracy*," Spencer corrected.

"I said *confederacy* and I mean *confederacy*. There are two governments operating in this house. And that's a confederacy."

Everyone was excited. It was open season on nerves, and we were suddenly a family of sopranos. Everyone's voice was so high pitched that when I asked Spencer to pass the salt, he asked me why I was screaming, and I thought he was screaming as he asked me why I was screaming.

This time Aunt Thelma met us at the game. She didn't like walking too much; there was always so much equipment to carry. Even in low heels, she found it difficult. When she was golfing, she always used a golf cart. The crowd at the game was enormous. It was a sell-out; that's what it would have been called in the pros where they actually sell seats instead of passing a hat. Parents of the Elks and friends and parents of the other teams in the league came. Sidney Polsky's tutor came. For Point Baldwin it was the seventh game of the World Series.

Mother called the team together in the dugout. We all felt a lot, so she said very little. "The fact is, fellas," she said, "that I really want to win this game.

I'd say that winning this game would be the second nicest thing in the whole world. The first nicest would be to be able to say that we played hard and honest and up until the very last out. And the whole time we didn't think with our feet."

Spencer smiled real big, which is unusual for Spencer. I often wonder if he got out of the habit when he had his braces. "You can do it, fellas," he said. And then he gave us our batting order. #3, Burser (3b); #10, Botts (2b); #7, Jacobs (1b); #4, Sylvester (ss); #6, Hersch (c); #2, Mark (cf); #8, Sonefield (rf); #12, Polsky (lf); #5, Simon (p).

Mother and Aunt Thelma had conferred and decided that letting Sidney start in a crucial game would be as beneficial to his development as losing weight had been.

The game actually got under way five minutes early because everyone was so ready and so excited and the bleachers so full that no one, not even the umpires, could see any reason for not starting. Waiting around is a sure nervous-maker. There was no score at all in the first three innings. And then we went ahead in the fourth. Hersch had struck out. I was next at bat and I got a single, which swelled to a double because their right fielder couldn't pick the ball up fast enough. To be able to get a hit in a pinch like that makes a guy feel like he invented success. Sonefield struck out, but Sidney got a single. His tutor cheered; his mother did everything but pass out cigars. Simon drove everything home with a high fly ball, which the Elks would have caught if they had not caught the jitters instead. None of the Bagels minded Burser's out because we were feeling good and comfortable; a three run lead can give you that good and comfortable feeling.

Temporarily.

The Elks chewed our lead down to two runs in the fifth inning. Mother noticed that Simon was tiring, and she went out on the mound to talk to him. The umpire stopped Aunt Thelma halfway there; Aunt Thelma looked deprived.

With our two run lead and Simon getting tired, Mother wanted to build up our lead in the bottom of the fifth. Botts was lead-off batter and got a double. Barry was up next, and Mother signalled for him to bunt; he took a good swing at the ball. The signal for bunting was for Mother to rub her nose and scratch her ear. Mother rubbed, and Mother scratched. Barry swung at one ball after another. He went out swinging: A, B, C; strike, strike, strike. Sylvester's hit advanced Botts to third, but both were left stranded because Hersch hit into a double play. So we finished the fifth inning by not improving our lead. It was obvious, though, that we would have had one more run if Barry had bunted because then Sylvester's hit would have given Botts passage home. Mother spoke to Barry when he came out of the batter's box. No one could hear what she was saying, but

it wasn't necessary. She was doing great imitations of herself rubbing her nose and scratching her ear. Barry looked over at his mother while my mother was talking to him. Then he smiled, shrugged his shoulders at his mother, and walked to the dugout. I don't think I've ever disliked a guy so bad. Much, much worse than when he called her Old Lady Bagel.

The leftovers of Simon's virus must have caught up with him in the sixth inning. He didn't seem to have the strength to finish his practice pitches. And then. And then he gave up the two runs that the Elks needed to tie up the game.

The bottom of the sixth and the bottom of our batting order. Me, first, then Sonefield and Polsky. I took the signal from Mother, swung and missed. Then I got three balls right in a row before I began hitting a long series of foul balls, which at least had the virtue of tiring their pitcher; he was beginning to lose stuff. I looked up at Mother for the little bubble of encouragement she usually gave us guys at bat, but she wasn't there. And then we all heard the noise, and the umpire called time out.

Mrs. Polsky had marched onto the field. Invaded the field. Mrs. Polsky was raising her voice and raising her arms and waving a copy of *Playgirl*.

"This boy," she yelled to the umpire as she pointed to Franklin P. Botts, "is creating a disturbance."

The umpire said, "Madam, you'll have to leave the field."

Spencer added, "Calm down, Mrs. Polsky. Please calm down."

The whole audience had moved to the stand behind our dugout.

"Calm down! I am calm," she shrieked.

The umpire said, "Madam, you'll have to leave the field."

"I warned you, Bessie Setzer, that I would put a stop to this if you didn't," she yelled at Mother and pointed to the magazine the whole time.

The umpire said, "Madam, you'll have to leave the field."

"I will not leave until this magazine is in proper hands."

"It's in proper hands right now. Yours," Mother said. "So, go already, Mrs. Polsky, and let us finish our game."

Mrs. Polsky wouldn't leave. It seemed as if she wanted to make a speech now that she had a platform. She didn't really have anything more to say. She just kept saying, "I told you I would put a stop to this." She seemed at a loss for words but not for time.

Spencer cupped Mrs. Polsky's elbow in his hand and led her from the field. "Come now, Sarah . . ." he said.

"Mrs. Polsky," she corrected.

Aunt Thelma shrieked, "Sarah Polsky, get up in those bleachers where you belong so that we can finish our game. You've delayed it long enough."

And that's how Mrs. Polsky left the game. With Spencer gently pushing her and *Playgirl* up the bleacher steps.

The game resumed. I walked. Sonefield and Sidney struck out. Simon, #5, was up next. Simon, #5, hit a home run and gave us a two run lead. Simon, #5, hit left-handed. Simon had never before been a switch hitter. Funny.

Funny, too, that Simon pitched left-handed against their three powerful left handers in the next inning. He held them to a single hit, and we won the game and the championship by the two runs batted in by Simon, #5. I was one of the runners brought home from my walk.

The team was jubilant. The whole audience swooped down onto the field like a huge mud sink being drained. Everyone was patting everyone on the back; Mother and Spencer must have felt like tympani.

There was only one person left in the bleachers, and it was Fortune Cookie Rivera. I left the mob on the field and walked to where she was sitting with her elbows resting on her knees and her chin resting in her hands. I got right down to the subject at hand. "Why would Barry sitting in our dugout watching an exciting baseball game buy a look at a magazine he already has a subscription to?" I asked.

"Because he knew that Mrs. Polsky would make a big fuss."

"Is that when Simon and Sylvester did it?" I asked.

She shrugged her shoulders. "Must be. They came out of the locker room right afterwards."

"Are you sure they did it?"

"How can I be sure? I couldn't count their teeth from up here. Could you?"

"I was trying to get a hit, remember?"

"Your mother didn't notice?"

"I guess not. She was pretty agitated about Mrs. Polsky. She doesn't know about the teeth anyway. She has a terrible time keeping them straight."

"And Spencer didn't notice either?"

"Probably not. He was spending his time keeping an eye on Mrs. Polsky and Botts."

"And your Aunt Thelma?"

"I doubt it."

"All I know is that neither of my darling twin brothers is clever enough to think of how they could pull the switch."

"Someone who knew that Mrs. Polsky would make a big fuss must have planned it," I said.

"Who knew?"

"Barry Jacobs, for one. His mother knew, and she tells Barry everything."

"And Botts knew, too. Your mother had called him and told him how upset Mrs. Polsky had been."

"But Barry Jacobs knew that he was costing us the game because he hadn't bunted. If you're sure your brothers didn't plan it, that leaves Barry and Botts as the only other ones who knew Mrs. Polsky would delay the game."

"And your mother," Cookie added.

"What's my mother got to do with this?"

"I just mentioned that she was also one who knew that Mrs. Polsky would fuss long enough for the twins to switch."

"Yeah, but Barry and Botts both had better reasons for wanting a victory."

"Don't get so excited. I just mentioned that if you're counting up all the people who had better reasons for wanting a victory, you have to add your mother's name to the list. That's all I'm saying."

"You're saying something else, too. Behind the lines, Cookie Rivera. You're saying that my mother is the only one who knew that we needed a left hander."

"I wouldn't say that. Spencer knew as well as your mother did. And your Aunt Thelma knew, too. Your Aunt Thelma even said, 'You've delayed the game enough.' And that makes a lot of Setzers who suddenly didn't notice that they had a left hander pitching instead of a right hander. A lot of Setzers."

"My Aunt Thelma is not a Setzer."

"I won't tell you what I think your Aunt Thelma is."

"And I won't tell you what I think your brothers is. Are."

"And I won't tell you what I think your mother is.

A Rebekah!"

"Nah! Nah! You just told me! Rebekah who?"

"I won't tell you *that!*" And Cookie walked away.
I left the bleachers and walked back into the
crowd, which was just beginning to show signs of
wanting to go home.

Everyone came into the house triumphant. I came
in worried. Dad was the only one to notice and the
only one to ask what was the matter. He had followed me up to my room and was standing outside
the door.

I answered the usual, "Nothing."

"Are you maybe disappointed that the season is
over?" ·

"Yeah, I guess that's it."

"It's not like losing a friend. Soon there will be
swimming," Dad said as he walked into my room.

"Yeah," I said.

"Well, Moshe, it was a great season," he said as he
sat on the edge of the bed.

"Yeah."

"Spencer tells me that you've become quite a little
ball player." He kicked off his shoes.

"Spencer tells you! That's great. That's just real
helpful. Why didn't Spencer tell me? I can think of
a few times it would have helped."

"I guess he figures that being good is something
you know by yourself. It would have been awkward

for him to tell you in front of everyone. It would have seemed that he was playing favorites."

I said nothing. Like Spencer I filled in the overlaps with a nothing vocabulary.

The silence thickened; Dad tunnelled through it with, "Well, you'll certainly still have enough to keep you busy, getting ready for your Bar Mitzvah and all. How are the Bar Mitzvah lessons going?"

"Not too bad since I've learned *fortissimo*. The rabbi doesn't look like he's hearing a heavenly choir, but at least now he seems as if he's closer to laughing than to crying."

Dad smiled. One of those smiles that is pushed from the inside; it started at his eyes and pulled his mouth upward.

"Speaking of Hebrew lessons," I said.

Dad said, "Yes." If there's anything that can make my dad happy, it is if you ask him some questions he can be an authority on. Sometimes I wouldn't ask him even though I knew that it would save me time and make him happy if I did, and I guess that shows I have a mean streak in me. But right then, I wanted to find out something.

"About the story of Esau and Jacob," I began.

"Yes," Dad answered, "the twins from the Bible. Genesis, Chapter Twenty-seven."

See what I mean about Dad being eager to show off to me about his knowledge? Everyone knows that Esau and Jacob were twins and that the story is in

Genesis. Only Dad would add the chapter number. But I went on. "Yes, the twins from the Bible. Genesis, Twenty-seven. You remember how Jacob disguised himself as Esau by putting on Esau's clothes and all, and how he stole Esau's blessing from Isaac, their father?"

"Remember? Of course I remember."

I continued being patient. "What I want to know is, did Rebekah, their mother, know about the switch?"

"Know about it? My dear young man, she gave Jacob the idea altogether. She choreographed the whole thing." That's another thing about my dad. He uses words like *sophomoric* and *choreograph*. He likes words a lot. Maybe they are a relief from numbers for him.

"What she did was pretty dishonest. How come she got away with it?"

"Because before she gave birth to the twins, Esau and Jacob, she received from God a message that told her she would bear twins and that the older, who was Esau, would serve the younger, who was Jacob." And then Dad quoted some passage of the Bible in Hebrew. He sure knows a lot, my father. He ended up by saying, "Rebekah knew that Jacob should have had the blessing; she merely helped arrange things to happen that way."

I paused a minute before I said, "Mother talks to God a lot. She's always saying things to that light fixture in the kitchen. Do you think she ever got a message back? Like that she should win the Little League championship? And that maybe she should put in a Jacob for an Esau?"

"I'm sure your mother wouldn't bother the Lord about Little League."

"She sure would! She even tells Him when I don't finish my spinach. 'For such an ungrateful child you cause green grasses to grow?' she says. You just don't listen to her, Dad. She's been bugging God about Little League ever since she became manager. You should have heard her when Spencer came down with the virus!"

"Well, son, your mother is an emotional woman. Whatever she does, she does with her whole heart and soul. And her heart is large, and I think that her soul is, too. And the excess spills out in talk. But I don't think she thinks that she is talking to God in that light fixture. She talks to Him quietly in prayer, and she doesn't bother Him about Little League or spinach."

"She thanks Him for every game we win!"

"She's not thanking Him for the game as such. She's thanking Him for giving her the strength and the stamina. She knows that she, not He, is planning the strategy."

"She plans strategy all right, but so did Rebekah."

"Your mother has been talking to God ever since we got married. However, I'm sure that if He ever answered back, it's been by answering prayers. Not *viva-voce.*"

More words. "Does *viva-voce* mean out-loud?"

"Very good," Dad said. Another thing about my dad. More than liking to show how smart he is, he likes me to show how smart I am.

"She keeps sending those messages, and I'm not sure that she doesn't think she gets messages in return. I wouldn't be surprised if Mother plotted a Little League victory the way that Rebekah plotted."

"If your mother plotted anything, Mark, don't you think that you would have found out about it? How can your mother keep anything from us? She wears her thoughts on her face like a cosmetic."

"She keeps things from us."

"Name one."

"I'll name one: the fact that my option price was eight hundred and she bought me for nine-twenty-five. The fact that she blackmailed Spencer into being coach. The fact that she knows I have a *Play-girl* magazine hidden under my mattress. How's that for one?"

"That would do for three."

"I can count."

"How can you say that she keeps things from us when you know all the things that you say she keeps from us?"

"She thinks she's hiding things from me, but I listen in."

"Why don't you listen in further and see if you

can discover what she's keeping from you now?"

Just as he said that, Mother's voice drifted upstairs. You can hear everything from anywhere in that house. Downstairs my mother was singing, actually singing, "Oh, it ain't gonna rain no more, no more . . ." She was singing *fortissimo*. Her singing told me two things: first, that she was no Barbra Streisand and second, that she was no Rebekah. I also remembered that she had said that winning would be the *second* nicest thing.

Dad quietly left the room.

After he left I noticed his shoes, which he had taken off; I picked them up and carried them into the office. The extension phone was in there. What would Hersch think of his Crescent Hill buddy now? I picked up the receiver and dialed the first three digits of Hersch's number. But I hung up. I picked up Dad's shoes again and took them into his room. If they had been any decent, normal style, I'll bet that I could have borrowed them.

I went to bed convinced that my mother was innocent. My father had convinced me. I wasn't sure how he had done it, but he had. I was also convinced that I had to tell Mother and Spence. It would cost us the championship, but I had to let them know. In a way, my telling would make me responsible for our losing the championship.

And there will always be people who will think that I wanted to tell to show Barry up because about now everyone knows how badly I wanted Hersch back. But I know that's not the reason because I never finished dialing Hersch's number. I never told Hersch about Barry then or ever.

It was a decision to do the right thing. It wasn't revenge; I could have gotten even with Botts, and never did. And it wasn't tattle telling. It was a decision I made by myself in bed that night after everyone thought that we had won the championship, and I knew that we hadn't.

15

EVEN THOUGH SCHOOL WAS OUT FOR THE YEAR, SATUR-
days still meant services at the synagogue. I sat alone
and walked out alone. In addition to wishing me
Good Sabbath as I left, the rabbi also wished me congratulations. I could hardly wait to get home to mope.
I moped around all the rest of the day. Mom kept getting called to the phone. Congratulations! Congratulations! Finally, she told me to stop moping around and
go read a book. That was her answer to everything:
go read a book. I got down the *Official Rules for
Little League Baseball* and looked for a loophole. I
couldn't find one. Mother was so happy that she was
bubbling somewhere in her soul. I couldn't puncture
that even though I knew that the longer I waited to

tell, the more deflated she would feel.

By suppertime I still hadn't told. Mother spooned out the goulash; its burnt flavor hadn't improved with age. I sang *Happy Birthday* to it, and Dad gave me a nudge under the table.

Talk about baseball never ends with the season. Especially in our house with our mother. "I sure would like to put Simon and Sylvester in the Tournament," she said. "But I guess it's not fair to the twelve-year-olds who are also good and next year it will be too late for them."

Spencer added, "They sure beat almost everyone I've seen in the League. Maybe the Bagels could sponsor four players. The twins deserve some special kind of recognition."

"I think so, too," Mother agreed. "If we can't get two extra places in the Tournament Team, what else do you think we could do for them?"

"How about giving each of them a sock in the nose?" I quietly suggested.

"Why would anyone want to do that?" Mother put down her fork and gave me a puzzled look. I knew that I was about to burst that bubble in her soul. But I knew that I better do it before too many more days of too many more congratulations.

"Didn't you notice that Simon pitched the last inning with his left hand? Didn't you notice that Simon took his last time at bat, batting left-handed?"

Mother squinted real hard. Everyone stayed quiet.

Mother changed her focus from space to Spence. "Spencer, which of those two boys is the left-hander?"

Spencer answered, "The one who is number 4."

Mother cocked her head to one side and said, "That's right. That's right. I *think* that's right." Then she went into the dining el and returned with yesterday's official records. She was nervous; she cleared the place in front of her by shoving the back of her hand against her cup and saucer. I knew how she was feeling; it's like hearing from some kids after a test about some question you can't even recognize, and then you have a sinking feeling because you realize that you may have skipped that whole side of the paper. It's panic until you get your paper back and see what it has done to your grade.

What a rattling of papers there seemed to be before she said, "Here. See. Simon was pitcher and was last in the batting order."

And Spencer said, "That's right. Simon is number five."

"And Simon also happens to have four teeth and Simon also happens to be the right-hander."

"What's the matter with his teeth?"

"Nothing is the matter with Simon's teeth. It's Sylvester who has the extra one. On the bottom. I couldn't see his teeth anyway."

Spencer leaned over and began to gently bang his head against the table. "What's with the teeth?" he

moaned. "What's with the teeth?"

"Teeth is the way you can tell Simon from Sylvester. All you have to remember is that Sylvester has five incisors on the bottom, and Simon has four and that is the opposite of their baseball numbers. Also, Sylvester has an *e* in it and so does *left*. Simon has an *i* in it, and so does *right*. It also helps to know that Simon has an *o* and so does *four*, the number of incisors, not the baseball number and Sylvester has an *e* and so does *five*, the number of incisors."

Dad was the only one who followed my explanation. He said, "Very good. Mnemonics. That's what it's called when you find little tricks like that to remember things." Even in an emergency my dad can't resist getting a little education into me. But he had understood. "What you are saying is that Simon, who wears number five shirt should have batted and pitched right-handed but instead batted and pitched left-handed?"

"That's right, Dad. Like Jacob and Esau."

"Are you convinced that your mother is no Rebekah?"

"Yeah, I'm convinced."

"From the Bible you quote when I need from the baseball manual," she said to Dad. Then to the light fixture she added, "You should please excuse the expression."

I caught Dad's eye and said, "See what I mean? She tells Him everything. All the time."

Mother said, "This discussion is no discussion; it is a crossword puzzle. Four down. Five across. Not a discussion at all."

Dad said, "Bessie, sit down."

Spencer popped up from his seat to grab the papers in front of Mother. And Dad added, "You better sit down, too, Spencer." Spencer sat. It was difficult for Dad. "What I have to tell you is . . . that what Moshe was trying to say was . . . that what may have happened yesterday was . . . to use plain, everyday language . . . Simon and Sylvester may have pulled a switch."

"Don't be silly!" Mother said. "I'm certainly no great authority on numbers like certain people in this house, but I do know a four from a five. Even on the back of a shirt, all wrinkled, I know a four from a five."

Dad said, "Isaac did not know Jacob from Esau when Jacob was dressed in Esau's clothes."

Mother looked up at the light fixture and said, "Again!"

Spencer shook his head. "How could they have done it? There was a huge crowd. The biggest they've had all season."

Dad answered, "For that information, you better ask Mark."

Everyone looked at me, and I was about to begin saying that it was Barry Jacobs' idea. But I didn't. Instead I said, "I think you ought to call Simon and

Sylvester, Barry Jacobs, and Franklin P. Botts. Call a meeting. They can give you all the answers. I'm not sure I can."

I had hardly finished saying it when Mother had taken down the phone book from the top of the refrigerator.

That evening they gave me money for a movie and enough for Hersch; they also gave me fifty cents for popcorn plus a ride for both of us to the shopping center where the movie was. Never before had I been allowed out at night to a movie without being accompanied by my parents. A double feature besides. One of those that always get circulated after the Academy Awards featuring in the one the male Oscar winner and in the other the female supporting star or some such combination.

Hersch's mother was supposed to pick us up from the movie. We waited for her in front of the theater, and it was then that Hersch mentioned baseball for the first time that evening. Between the popcorn and listening, we didn't do much talking in the movie. Hersch asked, "Do you know yet who's going to be on the tournament team?"

"I guess that will be decided this evening," I answered in a normal tone instead of a sneaky voice that would arouse his suspicions.

"I think that Barry should make it for sure; it would be great if both of us could make it."

Second chance. Some new, deeper voice (my own new voice?) told me to stay quiet, and I did.

Hersch added, "You know, Mark, you've come a long way; you're quite a ball player now. I'll bet if your mother weren't manager and your brother weren't coach, you'd be a choice candidate for the Tournament team."

That was a nice thing for him to say; it showed that he understood that having my mother as manager made me something less than my own person. I didn't answer except with nice thoughts. Then his mother picked us up.

Mother, Dad, Spencer, and Aunt Thelma were all sitting in the living room when I walked in. They were all examining fingernails or shoelaces or lint on the living room carpet. They had the look of losers.

"Well," I asked, "was it true?"

Aunt Thelma answered, "Yes, your mother just called and forfeited the game."

I walked over to my mother and put my arm around her shoulder, and she reached up and patted my hand. "Too bad, Mom," I said.

She looked up at me with eyes sad and moist. "Sometimes you just can't always tell about people." She swallowed her own private marshmallow, and Aunt Thelma made a sound that was somewhere between a shudder and a sigh. Mother said, "Where did I go wrong, Sam?" She was pitiful.

"It's all right, Bessie," Dad said.

"Did I make them care too much, Sam?"

"No, Bessie," Dad said. "The trouble didn't come about because the team cared too much. The trouble came because Barry couldn't stand being wrong and being a loser."

"But Botts and the twins were in on it even if they didn't plan it. They're all sour Bagels," I said.

"Botts and the twins made a mistake, but on the whole they've finished the season ahead of themselves. Botts has learned something about being open-minded, and the twins have learned something about not being led around. And as for Barry's being a sour Bagel, I'm afraid you can't say that. The truth is that Barry doesn't know what flavor Bagel he is. He is his mother's and his father's and his teacher's kind. Nothing but overlapping flavors. It almost wasn't his decision to pull the switch."

"If he planned it, it was his decision," Aunt Thelma said.

"Not quite. Botts' parents paint their prejudices on him, but at least they leave him alone enough so that he can wash them off every now and then. Barry never gets that chance; he's never alone. He's got no private picture of himself, only a public one," Spencer said.

"What do you know about Botts?" I asked.

He didn't answer.

Mother said, "Botts' prejudices are like bad manners. Like he never learned to eat with a knife and fork at home. He'll learn better."

"Little League was good for him," Aunt Thelma said. "In a way it was his first lesson in table manners."

"What do you know about Botts?" I asked Mother. Mother and Spencer exchanged a look before she answered, "What do you mean what do I know about Botts? I know that he's a terrific batter."

"What else do you know?"

"I *else* know that he's sorry for making us forfeit."

"Is that all you know, Mom?"

"What else is a mother supposed to know? Is she supposed to know what the *P* in Franklin P. Botts stands for?"

Dad offered, "I'm not too sure, but I think that the *P* is for *Playgirl*."

I let Mother think I didn't know that she knew about Botts; after all, Mother (and Spencer) had done that much for me. They had let me think they didn't know.

On Monday there was a small notice in the paper about the B'nai B'rith team forfeiting the game because of an illegal pitcher. They mentioned that the Elks had not protested but that the forfeit had been voluntary on the part of the B'nai B'rith. Mother and I spent that day at Aunt Thelma's, but even after supper the phone never stopped ringing. I answered and told them that Mom was in the shower, and she appreciated it.

Hersch and I were put on the Tournament Team. Some people think that I made the team because of my mother and brother, but I know that's not the reason, and so does Hersch. What we were, was leftovers. Again. Mother felt that she didn't have to punish Botts and Barry, but she also felt that she didn't have to reward them either. Hersch was catcher, and I played center field in the game we won and in the game we lost; Point Baldwin was wiped out at district championship, one less than Spencer's great year.

It wasn't so bad being a Tournament leftover. I got to see more of Hersch, at practices at first. And then because of Spencer I got to see him pretty often. All during the summer. Even before Barry went off to camp. One night after supper old Spence said to me, "Hey, kid, do you want a lift up to Hersch's house? I'm going up to Crescent Hill anyway."

"How will I get back?"

"I'll pick you up and bring you back."

"How will I know when you'll be bringing me back?"

"I'll send you a telegram! What do you mean how will you know? I'll drive to Hersch's and I'll honk the horn, and you'll come out to the car and I'll bring you back."

"How come you're doing this?" I asked.

"I told you, I'm going up to Crescent Hill anyway."

"How come?"

"Did I ask you why you're going up to Crescent Hill?"

"You didn't have to. You know that I'll be going up there to visit Hersch."

"Well then, don't ask me either."

How can you reason with a guy like that?

Spencer goes up to Crescent Hill a lot now. Sometimes he brings Hersch back with him. Usually when he picks me up to return me from Hersch's, there is a peculiar smell in the car. Hairspray. And the seat cushion close to the driver's seat is squooshed down. Spencer has quit picking on Mother. He whistles and hums a great deal. Her name is Faye; she also commutes to N.Y.U.

Hersch and I don't see each other as often as we used to, but he calls, and I call. Our friendship is pretty good now except for that small part about Barry. Like when a zipper gets broken and you repair it; it works all right, but there is always a fraction of an inch that's never quite on track, and you have to remember to be careful about that part. I noticed that Hersch is careful about that part, too. We never play the sarcastic game any more.

16

MY BAR MITZVAH WAS IN LATE AUGUST. EVEN AUNT Thelma helped bake for it (chocolate chips and brownies). Having to prepare for it was a good way for Mom to forget about Little League.

I never knew that I had so many relatives, and a Bar Mitzvah is a good way to find out; they all bring presents. My year was a big one for thesauruses: I got four. I checked at the bookstore about trading one in on a subscription to *Playgirl*. No dice. I also got three pairs of cufflinks, and I don't have a single one of that kind of shirt. Neither does Dad. I offered them to Spencer, but he hadn't run out of the cufflinks from his Bar Mitzvah yet. I went to the department store to see about trading them in on a subscription to *Play-*

girl. No dice. I figure that I'll save one for Sidney Polsky's Bar Mitzvah and one for Louis LaRosa's, except that Lou isn't Jewish.

My parents let me invite anyone I wanted to the party on Saturday night. They had almost everyone on the list already. I added Cookie Rivera and her brothers. Not Botts, who was away at camp anyway. So was Barry. I figured that it wouldn't hurt to have Cookie and the twins. And it was her first chance to see me without my braces. Of course, she never told me how nice I looked without them, but she noticed.

According to Hebrew Law, now I am a man. That is, I can participate fully in all the religious services. But I figure that you don't become a man overnight. Because it is a becoming; becoming more yourself, your own kind of tone deaf, center-fielder, son, brother, friend, Bagel. And only some of it happens on official time plus family time. A lot of it happens being alone. And it doesn't happen overnight. Sometimes it takes a guy a whole Little League season.